John Huntley Skrine

Joan the Maid

A dramatic romance

John Huntley Skrine

Joan the Maid
A dramatic romance

ISBN/EAN: 9783337049188

Printed in Europe, USA, Canada, Australia, Japan

Cover: Foto ©Andreas Hilbeck / pixelio.de

More available books at **www.hansebooks.com**

JOAN THE MAID

A Dramatic Romance

BY

JOHN HUNTLEY SKRINE

WARDEN OF GLENALMOND

AUTHOR OF 'COLUMBA,' 'A MEMORY OF EDWARD THRING,' ETC.

London

MACMILLAN AND CO.

AND NEW YORK

1895

TO A NAMESAKE OF
THE MAID'S 'SISTER OF PARADISE'
SAINT CATHARINE

The Saint who warred and rued I sang
    Thy woods among.
Among thy woods I heard the clang
Of Treason's gate, the trap that sprang,
When answerless to heaven uprang
    The Maiden's wrong.

Tale of the crown of womanhood
    I bring to thee,
Beside whose hearth, in lifted mood
Of commune on the Fair and Good,
I sat, and surelier understood
    What women be.

NOTE

THE tale of Joan here presented, though described as a Romance, claims to be true to history even in its detail. Those incidents of the play which have no place in the records have either been framed upon the model of actual incidents, or at any rate are in good accord with the known facts of the life. The part of the plot concerned with Raimond (of whom nothing is known beyond his name and office) will seem the least in keeping with those facts; yet hints can be adduced from the history enough to legitimatise the conception of his relations to the Maid, and of the abortive plans of rescue.

DRAMATIS PERSONÆ

CHARLES, *the Dauphin.*
GEORGES DE LA TREMOUILLE, *Councillor to the Dauphin.*
REGNAULT DE CHARTRES, *Chancellor, and Archbishop of Rheims.*
LE MACON, *a Councillor.*
DE GAUCOURT
DUNOIS
LA HIRE } *French Commanders.*
XAINTRAILLES
FLAVY, *Governor of Compiègne.*
RAIMOND, *Squire to Joan.*
D'AULON, *Maître d'Hotel to Joan.*
LOUIS DE CONTES, *Page to Joan.*
PASQUEREL, *Chaplain to Joan.*
CAUCHON, *Bishop of Beauvais (presiding judge in the trial of Joan).*
JEAN BEAUPERE
DE FONTE } *Assessors to Cauchon.*
GUY DE LAVAL, *a Nobleman.*
SIR JAMET, *a French Knight.*
FRIAR ROBERT, *a Preaching Friar.*
JACQUES (a Basque)
A SCOTTISH BOWMAN
A BRETON } *Soldiers.*
A GASCON
A MINSTREL.
ISAMBARD DE LA PIERRE, *a Dominican Monk.*
JOAN THE MAID.
MARGARET, *a Gentlewoman.*
MADAME BOUCHER, *Hostess to Joan at Orleans.*

Doctors, Notaries, French Lords, English Soldiers, etc.

ΕΓΓΥΣ ΕΜΟΥ, ΕΓΓΥΣ ΠΥΡΟΣ.

WHITE star of passion, fiery-pure,
    Death-lifted where thy-beam is thrown
    O'er England's field as o'er thine own—
Thy strifes are done : thy loves endure.

For thou hast all forgot the pain,
    Save when from thy large heaven is rolled
    On foe that slew, and friend that sold,
Thy pardon like a sobbing rain.

Or if some ghost of battle won
    Have touched thee, then on warring signs,
    Of Lion and of Lily, shines
One love, descending as the sun.

High Sister mine of Paradise,
    Blest singer were thy foeman's child
    If love-gift of a song beguiled
A smile of those unscorning eyes.

PROLOGUE

*The edge of the forest near Domremy.   A storm in
the distance.   JOAN seated.*

JOAN.   Milking time is it : but I have no heart
To rouse them from the brook.   How happy are they
Cooling their fetlocks in it,—all that's left,—
Their tails a-swing under the maple-bough.
Yea, let them bide awhile.   Yon thunder-cloud
Makes not our way.   'Twill slake a neighbour's field,
Not ours ; more pity for't !   Well, let them bide.
I shall not weary soon of watching them,
With so strange things to muse on, ah ! so strange.

How went the song I made me in the wood ?

Sings

Voices, voices, in the woodland calling !
          Heard we true ?
Nay, a wind that rose, and raindrops falling
          Where he blew,

Making patter all the leaves
Round the great oak's elfin eaves.
Ah! who troweth
What the tree saith when the vain wind bloweth?
Nay, but, heart, 'tis true.:
Hist! my heart, we heard it, and we knew.

Enter RAIMOND *on the other side*

RAIMOND.   I wonder if the hawk have built again
In the red fir.   He knew (the quick-eyed knave)
Raimond had gone to court this nesting-time :
He'd not dare else.   Who's yonder?   Yes, 'tis she,
Jacques' daughter: but how grown! and sweet (I'll
          swear it)
As when she witched me by their Dancers' Oak
Last summer.   Sooth, and there's a tale thereby,
A magic tale of her.   She looks it not:
So staid and simple: yet—   I'll try her.   Hist!
She is singing to herself.   She sees me not.

JOAN *sings*

Silver wings : an awful face in glory !
          Saw we so?
Nay, the tossing boughs of poplar hoary,
          All ablow
In the dazzle of sunlight
Off the shower-edge breaking white.

Ah! what wonder
If a maiden's fancy fleet beyond her?
Nay, but, heart, 'tis so:
Peace, my heart, we saw Him, and we know.

RAIMOND *approaches*

RAIMOND.   What sing you, Joan?

JOAN.   Ah! you, sir.   Nay, 'tis nothing.

RAIMOND.   Nothing? And so uptaken, as you sang,
You saw me not!

JOAN.   By watching of the kine
Belike I saw not.

RAIMOND.   Ay, belike, if kine
Were clouds or crows.   Joan, it is full a year
(By seeing you I know it) since I left
Our Domremy.

JOAN.   Where were you, sir, the while?

RAIMOND.   At court, beside the King.

JOAN.   The King! O then—

RAIMOND.   What then?

JOAN.   A thought. I cannot tell you what.

RAIMOND.   And why should Joan be thinking of
    the King,
You that have never seen him?

JOAN.   Never yet.

RAIMOND.   Nor ever will. The King, no hope has
    he

To see his faithful people here, the foe
So hedge him.

JOAN.   Does the King not trust in God ?

RAIMOND.   How know I ? Chief he trusts La
    Tremouille.

JOAN.   La Tremouille : what is it ?

RAIMOND.   Simple one !
But sooth, how should you know ?   A lord it is,
A lord that rules the kingdom and the King.

JOAN.   That should he not !   How dares he ?
        God is King
Over the King, none other.

RAIMOND.   Joan, how strange
You looked, how older of a sudden !

JOAN.   Sir,
What is it like to be at court ?

RAIMOND.   That you
Should ask it !   Not so wonderful, one half,
As I believed it.   But the times are sad,
And the King poor ; we know not where to turn.

JOAN.   Ah ! do ye not ?

RAIMOND.   O ho ! 'tis maiden Joan
Shall be our counsellor ! . . . I did not mean
To mock you : but such look you threw me then.

JOAN.   For Joan, or any child, could counsel you.
God's door is always wide.

RAIMOND.   Sooth, I bethink me :

You is it that would tarry at your prayer
Long when the Mass was done.   And once you looked
Even so, for I was watching, as you kneeled
Under the great Saint Michael.   Joan, do you
Remember that ?

JOAN.   My prayers are oftenest
Under the great Saint Michael.

RAIMOND.   Ay, they set
His picture there, the flaming eyes and sword,
Because through Him my grandsire beat away
Those English from our tower.

JOAN (*vehemently*).   As we shall beat them
Through holy Michael from all towers of France.

RAIMOND.   Ha ! Joan, now see I what you prayed
          for then ;
There comes the look again.   But dost remember
How I came near (I know not why : no prayer
Had I to make), but down I knelt beside you
Till yours was ended ?

JOAN.   And you had no prayer :
You, that will be a knight when you are grown,
And fight these English ?

RAIMOND.   Nay, no prayer I had ;
Only 'twas good to kneel beside you there,
As here is good to sit.

          (*Offers to make her sit down beside him.*)

JOAN.   O pardon me ;

That were too equal. 'Like may sit with like,'
Our mothers say.

RAIMOND. *My* mother, she that died
By trouble of these fightings, said the Saints
Look on us all as equal.

JOAN. Yea, the Saints.
But they who are not Saints may look on us :
And you are of the castle, not the cot.

RAIMOND. God made you for the castle, girl;
  I know it,
Yes, for I passed you once among the swains
When some ill jest had risen. How you flamed
And scorched them dumb! The anger in your
  eyes
Was like my lady mother's when they told
New woes of trampled France. I would you were
My sister.

JOAN. Noble sir, and how would I
That all the maids of France and all her men
Were sisters and were brothers to upbear
The woes of the one mother.

RAIMOND. All the men !
Our men are maids that turn unfoughten and fly
At a whirr of an English arrow.

JOAN. Shame to say it !
Was it not told us in the village here
Of those who set the Lily flag again

On Michael's pinnacle by the foam, and drove
Their navies seaward? Shame that you forget!

RAIMOND.   Ah! Joan, I do believe, to look on
    you,
Our maids are men to win fair France again.
Why so, a maid—it was a maid, they say,
(*Aside*) And nigh Lorraine . . . beside an oak-tree
    . . . why!
One of the people too. . . . (*Aloud*) Dost know the
    fable?

JOAN.   What fable, sir?

RAIMOND.   O but you know it well.
'A wife hath marred the realm, a maid shall make.'

JOAN.   Why do you call it fable?

RAIMOND.   Nay, I know not.
But when I told it at the court, they mocked.

JOAN.   They did right ill to mock it.

RAIMOND.   Joan, I vow,
If *you* were of the court they would not mock.
Saint Denis, no! they should not, if—

JOAN.   The court!
Ah me, God help me!

RAIMOND.   Maiden, what is this?
What was there in my saying to shake you so?
I would not jest at you, God knows, not I;
But if I touched unwitting—

JOAN.   Nay, not that.

Something came o'er—a fear—I cannot tell it,
Of days to be—

RAIMOND.   Fear! There be fears enough
This bitter time; France is a world of fears.
But wherefore words of mine—   O, if you have
Some trouble of your home, and help of mine
Or comfort might—

JOAN.   Ah! gentle sir, not now;
I know not if some other day.

RAIMOND.   Why then,
For sake of France and of our Domremy,
Yea, and for something, maiden, dearer yet,
Bid Raimond—there, your hand upon it. . . . Ha!

JOAN.   Why did you start?

RAIMOND.   Why? Let the clap make answer.
I had not thought the storm so near us.   There!
Stand wide.   Yon chestnut over us had the bolt.
And there again! We are in the heart of it, girl;
I saw the balled flame shiver adown an elm
To the earth, that swallowed it.   Dost *thou* not fear?

JOAN.   The fire of God? Why should we fear it?

RAIMOND.   Ay,
But the touch death. *I* fear it. Wide, I say,
Stand wide of the wood.   This drowning thunder-rain
Is kinder lodging than the covert.   Hark!
Why, said I not? there's the big limb of oak
I dragged you from beneath comes hurtling down

To brain us, were we under it. Heavens! and you
—What ails you, maiden? for you dread no more
This torment of the storm than if it were
Innocent sunshine, and you lift a front
Glad as a swordsman's when it peals to fight.
How can I choose but love you, being so brave?
Dear maiden, nay, 'tis truth. . . . Ah! what is this?
Merciful God!

    JOAN.   It strikes but whom He will.

    RAIMOND.   The miracle that you live to speak of it!
I saw you set on fire, the falling flame
Wrapping you like a robe. And you no hurt!

    JOAN.   Indeed I thought the bolt had slain me.

    RAIMOND.   Yea,
You thought so? Yet your eyes shone out of it
In joy as at a vision. Girl, you seemed
Like those who trod that furnace with the Lord.
The fire of God? But O! it came between.
I would it had not sundered you and me.

    JOAN.   O peace! I know not what you say. Fain
        would I
Walk with my God, though He should come in fire.
But let us part; the storm is less, the bolt
Has broke the cloud that bore. And peril's here
More than the bolt. Heaven keep you, sir . . . and all
The lovers of our France.   (*Goes.*)

    RAIMOND (*alone*). 'The lovers' . . . 'France' . . .

Less France, more love, were kinder.   Is she fair?
Not as our ladies of the court, and yet
When she uplit, how fairer!   Well, who knows?
Twain that love France to-day may come to-morrow
To love—   Yet ah! the sign that sundered us,
The fire of God, she said, the fire of God.

ACT I

SCENE I.—THE HALL OF THE CASTLE OF CHINON. NIGHT

The King, Nobles, Ladies of the Court

FIRST LORD (*entering*).   Hey day!   The blaze to-
night!   Our thrifty hall
And half a hundred lamps!   What riot's here
Of staid old steward Simon?   Friends, or is it
Some windfall to the starved exchequer?

SECOND LORD.   Ay,
Windfall enow.   The wind blows something hither:
But if to fill or empty—   You an hour,
A whole hour back at court, nor heard!

FIRST LORD.   'Tis you
I happen first on.

SECOND LORD.   Tut! your stable-lad
Would tell it, ere you loosed the stirrup.   Faith,
All day St. Maurice is a-buzz with her,
The crazed wench of Lorraine, if craze it be
That brings her, and not craft, as think the wise.

FIRST LORD.   Well, but her errand?

SECOND LORD.   Oh, a trifle, sir:
A gift she has from Heaven to make the King
Lord of his own, and bid these English pack.

FIRST LORD.   And do you credit her?

SECOND LORD.   Why, friend, my faith
Is—let her do the first, and I'll believe
She'll lightly do the second. . . . Hist! I see
La Tremouille's cousin not three heads away.
Well, yonder through the hall is gone Vendôme
To meet her at the stairfoot, much in pomp,
Mark you, and grave as if to pilot up
The Scots King's daughter, not a russet serge
And brown cheeks from the pasture. . . . There's
                  your squire,
Late too; but in good time, for is he not
Lorrainer? Ask him of his countrywoman.

FIRST LORD (*to* RAIMOND, *entering*).   Raimond,
      didst ever in your marches know
This will-be wonder-worker?

RAIMOND.   Who is he?

FIRST LORD.   He! Then Heaven bless thee,
      youngster.   Paired are we
For rawness. 'Tis a maid. But luck she brings
To save all France.

RAIMOND.   Then, man or maid, she comes
No hour too soon. And how then?

SECOND LORD.   Nay, but that's
Her secret.   Guess it you ; for she was bred
Under the shadow of your grandsire's tower.

RAIMOND.   So ?   And they name her ?

SECOND LORD.   Joan.   Or, Joan the Maid,
To give the style she favours.   Ah ! you know her.

RAIMOND.   A Joan there was among our folk : a
        child,
Scarce more, when I was with them—But, my lord,
What does the King in yon dim suit to-night,
And all the court so brave ?

SECOND LORD.   Come, let us guess it.
I'll say he tones his splendour, not to abash
This country-clad ambassadress of heaven :
A courteous reason.   You, rash boy, will say,
That prudent wight, our Dauphin's needleman,
Keeps back his braveries till more golden days
Arrive to pay his pains and—

VENDÔME (*entering with* JOAN).   Room ! my lords.
                    (JOAN *enters and pauses.*)

RAIMOND (*aside*).   Heaven keep us !   She ! or else
        my eyes are witched.

A LADY.   Poor child.   What ails Vendôme to
        leave her there
Daunted and mazed, and the King standing back
Hidden ?

SECOND LADY.   Not daunted.   Mark the pose of her,

And her eyes ranging like a carrier bird's
Searching its goal.

THIRD LADY.   Right: and she steers her to it
True as your homing dove.   She has found him, ha!
I marvel what's the message 'neath her wing.

> (JOAN *goes forward and kneels a little in
> front of the* KING.)

JOAN.   Heaven grant thee happy life, most gentle
King.

CHARLES.   Do not mistake, good maid.   Address
you there.

> (*Pointing to a richly-dressed courtier.*)

JOAN.   Ah! do not mock me, sire.   You are the
King.

CHARLES.   Mock me not you: look yonder; by
the robe
Discern him.

JOAN.   You would play upon me, sire;
I know not wherefore.   But the King are you;
To you it is God sent me.

CHARLES.   Damsel, rise.
Perhaps we did but try you.   Let it be.
Your name?

JOAN.   My name is Joan the Maid.   I come
To make you sure my God will have you crowned
At Rheims, through me His handmaid.

CHARLES.   Rheims!   (*To his courtiers*) The child

Dreams it a morning's pleasuring o'er the hills.
(*To Joan*) Heaven clear your wits, my girl : 'twixt
        Rheims and me
Stand half the English.

    JOAN.   I have said it, sire.
My God will lead you into Rheims by me.
. . . Ah ! they are laughing at me. Gentle Dauphin,
But you will heed my word, however these
Scorn it ; for you are ruler under God
Of France : you cannot scorn the weal of France.
O is it hard of credence ? Think you God
That hath such pity for our woeful land,
Will leave the true prince crownless, while the folk
Perish for want of him ? For were you crowned,
And on your brows the holy balm of France,
There is no might in any arm of men
To hold you from your kingdom.

    CHARLES.   Bravely spoke !
'Tis brave, but simple. Can the sacred oil,
Though every drop were thrice a miracle,
Help the poor prince who reaches for it across
The thorn-hedge of a score of fortresses ?
How seems it you, Sire de la Tremouille ?

    TREMOUILLE. My liege, I hold, as yesterday, with
        you
The sober counsel—to endure. Our strength
Is to sit still (my lord Archbishop's word) :

C

A weakly strength, mayhap : but therewithal
Our strongest.   Much ado to walk have we :
Your counsellor here bids fly.   But while she
     talks
The English hold of ours all Normandy,
Saving St. Michael's island-fastness, all
Loire side to northward : late on Rouvray field
Have stricken us hard, and now on Orleans
Their sword is falling—

    JOAN.   Falling !   Ay, 'tis falling.
O King, it has not fallen : it shall not fall.
I saw the sword of Michael counter it.
Ay, ye believe not.   But I saw it, I saw
On the altar step, beyond the darkening choir,
Great Michael, all his brand a blinding flame
Lit from his eyes : and, when I veiled my sight,
I heard him, ' Go, for this shall go before.'
Bethink thee, Dauphin : all the Holy Ones
Through the wide heaven are stirred with ruth ; the
     Saints,
And the great Charles, and Louis, and all that e'er
Wrought for dear France and loved her, on their
     knees
Plead at the throne's foot with the Lord of Hosts
To bid them arm for succour.   And ye delay !

                          (*A pause.*)
Ah ! Christ, that these may see it, as I have seen.

CHARLES. Sirs, give us space. We will have secret
speech
A moment with the maiden.

TREMOUILLE. Good my liege—

CHARLES. Nay, then, I well remember. Fear you
not.

(*Beckons* JOAN, *and goes apart with her
to a window.*)

FIRST LORD. How say ye? Did she plant that
arrow right?
She hath the King, I'll swear it.

SECOND LORD. Yes, the *King*.
Didst mark that creaming smile La Tremouille wears
Curdle on's lip? The tempest in the girl,
That fired the King, has soured the Councillor.

RAIMOND. Never I saw him stirred before to put
The Tremouille back so stiffly.

FIRST LORD. Bless her for't!
I'll vow the magic's white that works him thus.

RAIMOND. White! There was never black with a
white heart.

(CHARLES *and the* MAID *talk apart.*)

CHARLES. And that is true, maiden, and over-true.
Our hour's at darkest. Could I shut my eyes
To any ray, were it from God, and not—?
Nay, looking on your face I cannot say it.
Yet our wise heads mistrust your voices, Joan;

Some even yourself.   There would be surer sign
If 'twere of God.

JOAN.   What surer sign than this,
That France is dying, and God's angel sends
Word to her King to save her?

CHARLES.   To her King.
But are you sure then that he sent to me?

JOAN.   As that the King is speaking with me now.

CHARLES.   Is that so sure?   You doubted me at
    first.

JOAN.   Not for a moment, when I found your face.

CHARLES.   How knew you 'twas the King's?

JOAN.   God told it me.

CHARLES.   Why, then, He tells you all things.

JOAN.   No.   Yet all
I need to work His will.

CHARLES.   Then should He tell you
How to persuade the man He wills be crowned.

JOAN.   And that shall be, I doubt not.

CHARLES.   Happy soul,
That hears God's voice so clear, and cannot doubt.

JOAN.   *You* do not doubt it.

CHARLES.   Maiden, yet the man
Who does not doubt his God, may doubt himself.

JOAN (*starting and looking fixedly on him*).   'May—
        doubt—himself.'   Ah! then I see it, I see.
God showed your face: He shows to me your heart.

You do mistrust yourself the heir of France.
Out on her, wicked One! Alas, forgive me :
She was your mother in all but only love ;
Ill mother of France, ill mother of thee, but yet
Thy mother. O she lied, she lied in hate.
And by the Spirit of truth I tell thee true,
Her son thou art : thou art the seed of France.

    CHARLES. Ha! sayest thou, maiden ?

    JOAN (*seizing his hand*). Stay, and hear me out.
Now is it borne in on me like a light.
Prince, you have feared as I have, you have known
God's finger in a weight unbearable
Ruining the bowed soul under it, as have I.
Yea, this it was when at the feet of Christ . . .
Fallen on His altar-stone . . . in the lone shrine . . .
Under the banner of your fathers' wars . . .
Say I not true? Yes, yes—in that sharp hour
That woke the doubt and tore you with it again,
When first they brought to you my call—O this,
This was your prayer, that of His pity Christ
Would ease you of a realm not yours, or else
Write you His sure Anointed by a sign
Not to be questioned more. Behold! He heard.
Behold! the sign am I. Thou *art* the King.

    CHARLES. Maid, I am overborne and borne away
By a great wind of wonder.

    JOAN.   Let it bear thee.

It is a holy wonder, a wind of God,
Breath of His Spirit.

CHARLES.   Yea, for witness Christ,
That you have spelt the prayer none knew but He.

JOAN. And you to Rheims will go with me.

CHARLES.   Yea, yea:
Joan, you shall lead us, if my counsellors—
Nay, what have we with them? Henceforward I
Am mine own counsel: I will dare to rule.
. . . Ah! Joan, how sore a thing it is—to rule.

JOAN. Is it so sore? Nay, Dauphin, not for who
Is King but under Christ the very King.
But look upon your Lords; they are marvelling there.

CHARLES. Ah me, my lords! my lords and over-
   much!
Well, I will speak to them.

     My peers and dames,
Something has fallen 'twixt this maid and us
Beyond all measure of earth, not to be told.
For you—this maiden's message and herself
Judge with the best wit of your best. For me—
I have seen the hand of God: I am content.

Vendôme, we lodge the damsel in our court
Pending more counsel. You, my lord of Rheims,
Being spiritual, shall advise what means are best
To prove her to the realm's content.

REGNAULT.   My liege,
All my poor skill to serve you.

TREMOUILLE.   And all your court,
Believe it, gracious Dauphin, are one heart
To welcome your new hope.   Which Heaven
        confirm !

CHARLES.   We thank you.   Maiden, you are guest
        of ours,
But, if you would to lodging—

JOAN.   With your leave.
For I am very weary, as when the Saints
Have spoken with me.   All fair angels keep
Thy slumber, sire !

CHARLES.   Gentle my maid, and thine.

SCENE II.—THE GARDEN AT CHINON, OVERLOOKED
        BY A BALCONY.   EARLY MORNING

GUY (*from the balcony*).   Hillo ! sweet cousin, art
        abroad betimes.
What can my gallant want ?
RAIMOND (*below in the garden*).   To smell the
        spring.
GUY.   Lord ! 'tis a lovely answer, and demure ;
What's more, a truthful.   Yes, some flower of spring,
That opes at point of morning on the lawn

To bonny Raimond. Lily, violet, rose?
Or what's his fancy this week?

    RAIMOND (*picking a daisy, and holding it up*).
        Look, my coz;
Divine whose fancy this is.

    LOUIS (*entering balcony behind* GUY). Marguerite!
O ho! a hit, a hit for Raimond. Guy,
Swear now you never heard of Marguerite:
Nor even kissed her in the lilac bower,
When I—

    GUY.   You too, my mighty squire, afoot!
You four feet and a half of scandal. Fie!
Such naughty manners in the tender imp.
High time grave Father Etienne hear of this,
And counsel with the Countess: or—I have it.
Raimond, this gentleman shall be, they say,
Page of the Maiden Joan, Heaven help her! You,
For she's your countrywoman, warn her straight
What cockatrice she'll nurse. Off, mischief, off,
And see your lady's courser groomed against
Her tilting in the mead. I'll come, and end
My homily going.

    LOUIS.   O you never lack
Talk at your need: but mark, how one good word
Upset you, being true.

    GUY.   Come, must I beat you,
Child, into better manners?   (*Exeunt.*)

RAIMOND.   Gone, my luck
Be thanked.   She passes by this alley.   Yes.

(*Sees* TREMOUILLE.)

Beshrew my ears, then !

TREMOUILLE.   Ah ! your kinsman, sir,
Seeks you in haste : some service of the King's,
I take it.

RAIMOND.   Thanks, my lord.   (*Goes.*)

TREMOUILLE.   That clears the field.
This way the sibyl comes : and am I not
The sager escort ?   Let me squire her home,
And solve the engaging riddle—Joan the Maid.
I'll need endure her yet, since Aragon
Bargains his aid so stiffly.   But to march
In rank with Saints and Angels, Tremouille,
That suits you not : you cannot keep the step.
Come, there's a girl behind the prophetess ;
Unveil her.

Enter JOAN

TREMOUILLE.   Give you a good morrow, Joan.
You walk right early.

JOAN.   From the Mass, my lord.

TREMOUILLE.   Indeed you fail it seldom.   You
      will judge
Our Court too scant of worship.

JOAN.   Theirs the loss,
My lord, and all the kingdom's.

TREMOUILLE.   We will mend,
Exampled thus.   How likes it you at Court?

JOAN.   Right ill, right ill.

TREMOUILLE.   So? yet you bear yourself
Well, damsel, to a marvel.   Pardon me,
I speak but after Queen Yolande.

JOAN.   My lord,
I have only borne me as my nature is.

TREMOUILLE.   Nature is noblest manners then.
       But why
Mislike you so the Court?

JOAN.   Because the Court
Is not the Camp.   O, there, I should be there!

TREMOUILLE.   You shall, when speaks the Church.

JOAN.   'Tis long to wait.

TREMOUILLE.   Yet, damsel—

JOAN.   Pray you call me simple Joan,
My lord; I am not gentle.

TREMOUILLE.   Why, for that,
There are of us, if so the King inclined,
Would have you gentled ere your enterprise.

JOAN.   You do me wrong to speak it.   Who am I?
God's voice to-day for France, another while
A village maid again.

TREMOUILLE.   And do you think,

When our good hopes in Joan are fruit, the King
Will let you from him?

JOAN.   Yes, how else?

TREMOUILLE.   And you
Would go from Court to cottage?

JOAN.   O how blithe!

TREMOUILLE (*aside*).   She means it.   Need I fear
    her?   (*Aloud*) I perceive
We courtiers find no favour in your eyes.

JOAN.   My lord!

TREMOUILLE.   I mean you think us adversaries,
And hinderers of your counsel.   Do you not?

JOAN.   Indeed I thought you gave it little help.

TREMOUILLE.   When churchmen are so tardy,
    men of state,
Whose task is not the spiritual assay,
May be forgiven demur.   Besides, at Court
(Ask your own knowledge) there are nice regards
Of person, time, mood, favour, interest.
We move to action through such winding ways
It spreads the journey.

JOAN.   Will those English wait
Because your ways are winding?

TREMOUILLE.   Joan, the fault
Lies not with me.   You do not know the Court,
The maze of doubling passages and doors
That keep their secret.   There be keys, O yes!

But could you handle them, unhelped? I vow
My caution, tho' you count it for mislike,
Shall bring your counsel by a nearer road,
Would you so trust me.

   JOAN.   But there needs no trust.
God's is the counsel; Joan is ready here
To go when ye believe. Why will ye not?
The Dauphin did not doubt me.

   TREMOUILLE.   Ah, but he—
Joan, let me praise your conquest. Wonderful
Your instant mastery of our prince's heart!
You may do much with him,—yet (have I leave?)
—Nay, you have marked it, how he balances
Between advisers, this way, and now that.
Things would go swifter, could his counsellors
Agree without the chamber-door.

   JOAN.   My lord,
He is the prince; he has the Spirit of God.
Shall we not let his own heart counsel him?

   TREMOUILLE. Which is, let Joan the wise be
     counsellor,
The rest be dumb.

   JOAN.   I am not counsellor:
I am not wise: I only heard of God,
And came to tell him. O that all were done,
And I beside my mother's fire again!
Great sir, in God's name, do not daunt him, you.

TREMOUILLE.   Why, Joan, I will not.   I am cured
  of fears
Myself, if you are proven by the Church ;
And give my voice with yours, tho' something wronged
(Confess) by your mistrust.

JOAN.   I'll beg of you
A thousand pardons for it, if your word
Will stead me now.

TREMOUILLE. Well, that is fairly spoke.
And may our concord prosper !

JOAN.   As I pray.
But I am stayed for, and beseech your leave.

TREMOUILLE.   Fair day to you ! (*Exit* JOAN.)
      Now, what to make of this ?
What is she seeking here ?   A woman has
Her price, like every man ; but tell me Joan's !
. . . I like her none the better.   Shrewdness self
Is our sweet rustic ; in the game of Court,
And playing with our Kingling as the stake,
I dare not grant her odds.   Well, Aragon
Fails : to it, Joan.   Your boast is still to prove :
It may miscarry—Tremouille there to help.

SCENE III.—A Street in Orleans. The Fort
'London,' built by the English, is seen in
distance. Soldiers and Citizens on Benches.

A Breton.   Art early off the wall, old Jacques,
    to-day.
What's fallen to bring thee?
    Jacques.   Fallen?   I think it be
That hundred-pound-weight pebble we let fall
Slap in the London's mouth, sirs, plump and true
On her big bombard's nozzle.   After that,
Was quiet.   Drop a plum in a brat's mouth,
You stop the bellow: Peter's plum did hers.
They're mute as mice an hour long.   'Go, my lads,'
Cries Peter, with a grin, 'a score of you,
And stretch your legs at ease.   The Godons there
Will want no more of us this afternoon!'
Come, sit you down, and drink stout Peter's health.
    Breton.   St. Denis keep him ever a clean eye.
And yet I'd rather than a pair of hits
See the cock swing on steeple, and the wind
Ferrying our beef up river.
    Jacques.   Fill, my friend.
If we must eat the less there's drinking still.
    Scot.   Not long that either.
    Breton.   When the food is out,

The fight's out too.   There are pinched bellies here,
Mark me, would sell us for a bellyful.

GASCON.   The knaves that battered the com-
    mandery door.
Give me the piking them !   'Twould save the meat
Of honest fellows with a pair of hands,
To stay rogue mouths that fashion.

MINSTREL *enters singing*

. . . the arrow, the arrow,
The wing and the sting of the arrow.

GASCON.   Hark ye now :
The lazy, crazy knave that gives the folk
Faint stomachs with his drone.   I'd have the rogue
Whipped out of town and sent to earn his crust
Harping to Godons.   Hunger blight 'em both !
Have at you, rascal.   (*Moves to strike him.*)
    SCOT (*interposing*).   Nay, that shall ye not.
Let the poor singer be.
    GASCON.   What's he to you, then ?
Thou'lt claim no kin in him, that art not French.
    SCOT.   I know not : there's a breath of mountain
        song
Comes when I hear him.   A good music, sirs :
'Tis sad but gallant, and it stirs the blood
More than a merrier.   O the times have been

My mates and I have harried English ground
To even its like: 'tis our glen music, friends,
Wail of the wind in't and the river's wrath.

    JACQUES.   Ods! bowman Scot, didst ever loose
         till now

So many words at once? Wert wont to keep
More shafts than words in quivers.

    SCOT.   More's the thrift.

    JACQUES.   Belike. Well I strike thy way: let us
         hear him.

Sing us the ballad you were trolling now.

    MINSTREL.   It will not please you, masters.
        'Twas but made

For womenfolk and babes,

    JACQUES.   Sing out and fear not.

            MINSTREL *sings*

    'There's a hum in the air.
    Is it honey bee there,
And the winter wind cold on the meadow?
    O mother, what fled
    On the wing overhead:
Is it swallow went by with her shadow?'

    'Ah! no and no.
    Shelter thee low,

Child, from the wing of the arrow, the arrow,
The wing and the sting of the arrow.'

'Is there bread nevermore,
Nor on board nor in store,
And wee Janet afaint for the hunger?
O when and O when
Comes father again?
She will die if he tarry the longer.'

'Cease, my boy, cease:
God be your peace!
Father he lies with the arrow, the arrow,
Fast in his bosom the arrow.'

GASCON.   There! said I not?   What does he
    daunting babes
And womenfolk in that sort?
JACQUES.   Hold a bit!
He's yet an arrow of his own in's case;
Canst see it by his eyes.   Come, let it fly.

MINSTREL

'Ah! woe and ah! woe.
If the father be so,
Then who will be succour to-morrow?'

'Nay, child, be you brave:
When the man cannot save,
Shall the woman be succour in sorrow.

D

O a virgin will tread
The flying asp dead :
O a maid shall have might on the arrow, the
    arrow,
The flight and the bite of the arrow.'

JACQUES.   'Fore God, a gallant music, as you said,
Friend bowman.   Maid—the Maid !   Luck send her
    quick,
But (curse the luck) she tarries.   Pass a week,
And, friends, we'll have clean teeth in Orleans.
    GASCON.   Great thanks, to help us when they've
        picked our bones !
'Tis 'coming, coming, coming.'   Let her *come*.
    A VOICE IN THE CROWD.   She comes !
    SOLDIERS.   Who says it ?
    FRIAR ROBERT (*stepping out*).   I !
    SOLDIERS.   How know ye that ?
    ROBERT.   As all may know it who will.   When
        man has shot
His last, 'tis then we'll hear God's quiver rattle.
And, brothers, is there left one bolt in yours ?
    GASCON.   Ye preaching fool !   Is that your news ?
        Be hanged,
You and your sermon in your cowl-string.   Off !
    BRETON.   Shame !   He's the stoutest heart within
        the gates.

Stand to it, Brother Robert, preach it out.
Sirs, if we be not fallen in hands of God,
Ill fall is ours, I trow.

ROBERT.   Ill fall indeed.
But in the Lord's hands are we fallen.   I know it.
There came such brightness on me when I woke,
And after what a dream!

WOMAN.   Nay, tell us that.

ROBERT.   I dreamed I wandered on an endless
        plain
All in a mortal terror; for a cloud
Of loathly hawks, a hundred, following wheeled,
Darted, and struck, and struck: and as I might
With hand and arm I fought and fended me,
But still they stooped and struck, till sick I grew
For the long horror, and my arms as lead
For labour.   Then, and when I thought to swoon
And let the fierce beaks end me, lo! the plain
Was shocked with a clear trumpet, and all the fowl
Screamed and went up and hung a moment, and
        then
Shot like a volley of arrows along the wind
Off into dusk and silence.   And I saw
A broad and silver star that, nearing, rose
A pillar of white fire, and last a face,
A presence, horsed or winged I know not—Ha!

        (*A bugle note at the head of the street.*)

WOMAN.   Look if he have not fallen a-heap.   He
    thought,
Poor soul, it was his trumpet blowing again.

JACQUES.   Well, 'tis not blown for nothing.   See
    the folk
Flocking this way together; ods my life!
But there's Sir Jamet, and he's back from Blois.
Ho, ho! the news.

HERALD.   Good people, pray you keep
Silence to hear Sir Jamet make report.

CROWD.   That will we.   Brave Sir Jamet!   Hear
    him, hear him.

SIR JAMET.   Soldiers and men of Orleans, dear
    my friends,
Good cheer.   I bring you from the General's door
(His wish: he would not let you wait one hour)
The royal message.   Thunder it you abroad,
And make yon English quake behind their towers.
The Maid is proven.   The Maid has ta'en the march.
          (*Shouts, ' Long live the Maid !'*)

ROBERT.   God, Thou art just.

WOMAN.   O is it sure, is it sure?

SIR JAMET.   Good dame, and would I ride my
    horse half dead,
And race 'twixt English towers in open day,
And take a bolt-head on my saddle-leather
And twain upon my hauberk's ribs, to bring

False news or doubtful?   No, she comes, she comes.
She tramples, while we talk, the road of Blois.
From the first hill I watched her banner spring
White from the gateway, under it a star
Of armour, and a wind brought up the chant
As from an army's throat forth-speeding her.
And then I turned and spurred for all your lives.
Hold out one daylight more, and France is ours.

    JACQUES.   Hold out a hundred, now the Maid's
      on horse.
This makes the blood run lusty.   I could swear
I'd dined on honest beef a fortnight.

    BRETON.   Peace,
Old talker.   Good Sir Jamet, tell us more.

    SIR JAMET.   With a right merry heart.   What
      would ye hear?

    WOMAN.   How looks she then: and is she verily
      like
The blessed angels?

    SIR JAMET.   Sooth, and how should I
Be judge of that?   Unless indeed to be
Most woman is most angel.   So, 'twere true.
When I have done, ask holy Robert there
Whether she feature angel.   But for me,
Not till these eyes must close on women and men,
Nor haply after, if God open them,
Shall I behold a sight so wonderful.

BRETON.   Is she so fair?   This was not told us.

SIR JAMET.   Nay,
My word was 'wonderful.'   I said not 'fair.'
If she be fair as men call fair of face,
Scarce I bethought me.   Truth, a bloom she wears,
Flower of the blowing field and open sky,
That mates the shine of the black locks above.
And shapely is she made of limb; and treads,
Like roe-deer, strong and supple.   But to tell
Of features—friends, I knew, I saw but one.
For when she spake with mine own self that once,
Bidding me tell you be of cheer, her eyes,
All tears with her o'erflowing pitifulness,
All fire with that vast wonder of her faith,
These were the Maiden, and I saw but these.

    WOMAN.   And you have told it us right well, Sir
        Jamet.
Praise God, she verily is the Angel Maid.

    BRETON.   Yet she's but woman, and unmeet for
        arms.
How will she fare in wars?

    SIR JAMET.   O then I would
Ye had seen her on the muster-field of Blois,
With what a seat she rode her destrier out,
Coal-black and tall and hot, Alençon's gift,
And prouder than to bear a prince: for he,
When one brought forth her banner, and she reached

To take it, and he saw that first of beams
Fan the gold broideries into sparks, and set
The lilies tossing on the dimpling white,
Upright he reared and wheeled and gambolled from it
So riotously, we feared.   But she with never
A shake in the clear voice said, 'Turn me there
The flag-beam, let him look upon his God.'
(For on that side was God the Father woven,
Poising the world on palm, and underneath
Twain angels held to Him the lily of France.)
Sirs, the strong beast beneath her, when he saw it,
Stood fast and trembled; then he reached his neck
Forward, as if he wooed a master's touch,
And softly bore her towards it, and she took.
O had ye seen her take it, had ye seen
The shining of her face!   'Fore Christ, I know not
What angels be, yet if God bade one go
To war for holy France, an angel's face
Could light but with her gladness.   O she caught,
She kissed the staff, she kissed the hem.   The steed
Flung up the white star on his front to heaven,
And neighed for trumpet.   Round she reined him
          there,
And shook the pole, and swung the folds abroad,
Crying, 'The banner of France, the banner of Christ:'
And pricked him to career: and down the host,
The steely-billowy seas of armoured heads,

Went onward bounding, as a barque that strains
Across a racing seaway, dips and rears
Its snowy pillar of sail : for o'er the Maid
That shining banner of the weal of France,
Lifting and dipped and lifting, seemed to blow
Filled with our blasts of shouting : and drooped at last,
Pausing, to drape her sun-bright side, and kiss
The flushed girl-cheek and bright locks bare of helm,
And glory of her raptured maidenhood.

Ah ! but I cannot tell it as I saw,
For fulness of the heart.   Yourselves will see.
   CROWD.   Long live Sir Jamet !
   JACQUES.   Round me, fellows, ho !
We'll lift him on my target shoulder-high
And bear him to the rampart.   There we'll shout,
Till Talbot's sick for spite, ' She comes, she comes.'
                       (*Exeunt omnes.*)

SCENE IV.—OUTSIDE THE CHURCH OF SAINTE
CROIX IN ORLEANS

JOAN *enters, following a procession of* PRIESTS, *who
chant*

Mary, Maiden erst on earth,
Mother of the saving Birth,
   By the Maiden shield us.

Friend of all that virgin be,
Might of thy virginity
   Through the Maiden yield us.

Michael, in the angel war
First of all that warriors are,
   Hear us O, and heed us.
Ghostly Captain, Lord of Strength,
Draw from sheath the sword at length,
   Sword of heaven, and lead us.

PRIESTS *and* JOAN *enter the church.* PASQUEREL *and*
   D'AULON *remain without. Enter* RAIMOND.

RAIMOND. Most timely met with, Father Pasquerel.
I have not come astray. And D'Aulon too.
'Tis the Maid's household gathered. Comes she here?
   PASQUEREL. Why, sir, we wait her now. She hears
     within
The Mass at the great altar.
   D'AULON.   After that
Shake loose your blade, young sir, and look for deeds.
   RAIMOND. Ah! tell me that. I come in time,
     though late.
   D'AULON. Truth, and I marvel that I see you now.
You came not with the Maid, nor came from Blois
With us that fetched the succours.
   RAIMOND.   No, for lack

Of the King's leave.   I asked of Tremouille;
And he was bland as ever, and helped me nought.
And then of Regnault, he that fumbled so
In this despatch of succours.   Last I won
Cold leave, and spurred to catch you : saw you
          pass
(And marvelled) thro' the forts without a blow.
I breathed my horse behind a copse, and ran
The hazard.   Sirs, they sent me never a shaft !
What ails those English ?

    D'AULON.   'Tis the Banner, sir :
The Banner, and the Maid that's under it.
They say she's sorceress ; that we fight not fair
To use her magic.

    RAIMOND.   Sorceress !   Villain word.
But ah ! they have not seen the face of her.

    D'AULON.   Nay, but they have, and near.   She
          stood to speak
At the Fair Cross where ends the broken bridge :
Glassidas mounted the Tourelles and mocked ;
Bade her go mind her cows, and called her—Faugh,
God pardon that I came so near to say it.

    RAIMOND.   Is Glassidas his name ?

    D'AULON.   Why no, but near
As you can frame it on a civil tongue.

    RAIMOND.   Glassidas : Glassidas.   Heaven send
          we meet !

D'AULON.   Heaven send you elsewhere.   He's a
   brawny knight,
Ten summer stouter than your sapling arm.
Nay, colour not so hotly.   Where's the shame?
I am older in the wars, and spoke but sense.

RAIMOND.   'Tis anger, if I blushed.   But shame
   there is
To put a shame upon her.   Sorceress! ha!
To see, and yet defame her!

D'AULON.   Be content.
Their lie will serve our turn, so scares it them,
And robs their hearts of pith.   But I must hence:
And, being of her escort, you may learn
From Pasquerel where we lodge.   (*Exit.*)

RAIMOND.   Good Father, why
Stayed you without?

PASQUEREL.   She bade me wait for you.

RAIMOND.   She!   But none told her I should
   come.

PASQUEREL.   She bade
Await you by the church and bring you home.
I know but this.

RAIMOND.   Strange. . . . And it pleases her
To have me of her train?

PASQUEREL.   'Tis ordered so:
And you are very welcome, as I think.

RAIMOND.   Ah! . . . And why think you that?

PASQUEREL.   A child can know
What likes her or mislikes, so frank is she.
    RAIMOND.   Said she not aught?
    PASQUEREL.   No more than I have told.
But she can tell you all she will: they come.

PRIESTS *come from the church, chanting*

> Lord, that with the viewless blow
> Quellest fury of the foe
> And the arrows of their bow,
>   Thou to battle gird us.
> Lo! the armour of their trust
> And the sword of them as rust,
> And their boasting in the dust
>   Break.   The Lord hath heard us.

    JOAN (*seeing* RAIMOND, *who approaches and salutes
        her*).   Ah! true Sir Raimond, you are wel-
        come here.
Now are we mustered all: how glad am I!
I knew they could not keep you.
    RAIMOND.   Maid, the King—
    JOAN. Nay, could I doubt it?   See, 'tis our
        Lorraine,
Maiden and man, in arms at last.   O how,
Old comrade, could I battle till you came?
But now—(*to her train*)—sirs, welcome you this
        gentleman

As of our band, and bring him where to rest:
I know he has ridden apace. (*To* RAIMOND, *who
begins to speak*) Nay, tell me not.
      (*Exeunt* RAIMOND *and all but* PASQUEREL.)
Kind Father, wait a little yet: I'll talk
Three minutes with the children.
    (*Goes to a group of children on steps of church.*)
                    Sweet my friends,
You were not kneeling at my side to-day.
What hindered you to follow?
    ROSE.   I would come,
But Lilien daunted us.
    JOAN.   . How did she that?
    LILIEN.   It were too bold in us.
    JOAN.   You thought not so
Fore-yesterday, at Vespers.
    LILIEN.   *Then* you took
My hand, and made me come along with you.
But now—
    JOAN.   Well, now?
    LILIEN.   You arc so grand, and we—
    JOAN. Out on you! Will you wrong me, child,
      because
I cannot go to war without a horse?
I am your sister of the cottage roof;
And, little sister, I would rather sit
And sew with you, or drive the kine with you,

Than ride the tallest horse in all the world,
And live among the dreadful wars. Alas,
I am myself a child to those strong men,
Yet cannot be with children, save at prayer.
You will not grudge me that much.

    ROSE.   O no, no.
We'll come to-morrow again and every day.
We all do love you.

    JOAN.   Kiss and part, my rose.
You too, sweet rose-bud (*to younger child*). I must go
    to rest
Like any child, at noon, so tired am I.
There'll be another ride ere night (who knows?)
For stout Rolande and me. What, wilt not part,
Rose-bud? Then, Father, she must guard us home.

          (*Exeunt* JOAN *and* PASQUEREL *with the*
          children.)

SCENE V.—AFTERNOON OF THE SAME DAY. ROOM
    ON UPPER FLOOR OF MADAME BOUCHER'S
    HOUSE IN ORLEANS.

LOUIS *fitting out a helmet. Enter* MARGUERITE *behind
    him, and watches him.*

    LOUIS. There now, but that goes bravely! Tho'
    the plume

Should have been fuller. Yet the golden skein
Sets it right well. . . . There'll be no boys, I doubt,
With Talbot yonder. Still, 'tis knightly work
Guarding the banner, if she grudge me not.
O 'tis a bonny helmet !

MARGUERITE.   And I fear
Will give your honour headache.

LOUIS.   Marguerite ! You !

MARGUERITE. Strange : is it not? And in my
    kinsman's house.

LOUIS. No ; but how came you in ? I heard
    you not.

MARGUERITE. Great sir, your pardon then if *I*
    heard *you ;*
Your worship was so rapt upon your gear.

LOUIS. Well, what care I ? A bonny helm, I
    say.

MARGUERITE. And bonnily befits—O ho ! but
    what ?
How comes this silken skein about the crest ?

LOUIS. It is her favour.

MARGUERITE.   Hear him, rare my knight !
Is fifteen span or something more, and wears
His lady's favour o' casque ! But tell not me :
Or I'll give out I saw you pillage for it
Your hostess' aumry. Fie, the vanity !

LOUIS. O madam, you are mighty pleasant, you.

But ask herself.   Even now she gave it me,
Because I begged to wear her cognisance.
'Tis the self silk that the loomwomen wove
Into the standard's blazon : this was over ;
And this she chose, ' For you are sworn,' quoth she,
' Knight of the Banner of France.'   How say you now ?
 MARGUERITE.   A toy, a toy.   What cares she for
  a child ?
Favour !   I have more her favour than yourself.
 LOUIS.   Ah, so ?   How see you that ?
 MARGUERITE.   Why thus I see it :
No sooner come, she took me by the hands,
Looked in mine eyes, then kissed on either cheek,
' First, for you are my hostess kind,' she said,
' And next, for you were christened Marguerite.'
You kissed she never : no, on neither cheek.
 LOUIS.   Ah ! but how know you that ?
 MARGUERITE.   The innocent !
He hide the greatness !   Why, were Louis dumb,
It would be blazoned on his cheek a month,
And every curl would blab it.
 LOUIS.   Witty again.
But still your favour counts not.   You are girl :
While I am—
 MARGUERITE.   Boy.   I'll say it for you,—Boy,
That would say ' man ' and dared not.
 LOUIS.   There, have done.

For ever fleering at my fourteen years,

Till I am sick.   And you have missed the tale.

    MARGUERITE.   What tale?

    LOUIS.   The words she spoke in granting it.

You'd give her one kiss back to hear it told.

    MARGUERITE.   I love her every word.   Come tell

        me this.   (*Sits down by him.*)

    LOUIS.   Not I.   Besides, what cares she for a

        child?

What says she, worth your hearing, to a boy?

    MARGUERITE.   Nay, then, dear Louis, I repent

        me: see.   (*Kneels to him.*)

Your pardon that I so torment you.   Yet

Should I have teased you save I loved you well?

    LOUIS.   Then will you call me 'child' again?

    MARGUERITE.   O never!

I'll say you are a gallant gentleman,

That will be older, please the Saints you live,

And two spans longer—There again!   Forgive.

    LOUIS.   Well then, this once.   But sit we close,

        speak low.

Behind yon door is she laid down to sleep,

And, Marguerite, this is but for me and you.

    MARGUERITE.   Yes, yes.   When did you ever

        know me prate?

    LOUIS.   I have only known you, Marguerite, these

        four days.

E

Well, when she brought it out, 'My son,' she said
(Calling me thus, though scarce your age is she),
'You cannot wear a cognisance of mine
And be my knight, for there can never be
A knight of mine :' (now pray you, wherefore that?)
'But, Louis, be content; for you shall be
The Standard's Knight, and that is Knight of France
And of the Holy Will.   So take for yours
A cognisance of the Banner, golden thread
That wove the blessed sign we conquer by,
To bind your heart up with the thing you guard.
And, Louis' (here she all but whispered it),
'You have so many years to fight for France :
My time is short.   But you, when I am spent,
Wear you this favour still, but near your heart,
Secret, and pray for her who gave it you,
And war for France for whom she gave it you.'
Thereat she turned away, but I am sure
She wept, as I, God wot, was nigh to weep.
There, Marguerite : is my favour worth your two?

 MARGUERITE.   I fear me, by the envy that I feel.
'Twas sweet and passing sweet.   But then, 'My time
Is short.'   What means she by 'My time is short'?

 LOUIS.   Well, is it natural for a maid to fight?
She cannot do it long.   She'll fight, I think,
And drive the English, crown the King, and then—

 MARGUERITE.   Ah! yes; what then?

LOUIS. Why then—

JOAN (*from the inner chamber*). Ho! there,
    without.

LOUIS. Whew! She has waked. Alack, and she
    so tired!

Now, Marguerite, was it I that—? Madam, here.

JOAN (*entering*). Ay, here: and, wicked boy, how
    could you do it?

LOUIS. I am vexed of your awaking.

JOAN. There's the shame.

Blood of our France a-spilling, heartless one,

And not to wake me, you!

LOUIS. Lord save us, Maid!

Why—how—what—

JOAN. Prating, while the Frenchmen bleed!

Quick as you may, run, bring me round the horse,

Saddled; and this time, mark me, nought forgot.

Off! (*Exit* LOUIS) And, dear Marguerite, help me
    close my mail.

There, so it clasps,—nay, so. Ah! quick, be quick.

'Tis Louis' work, but he must bit Rolande.

Heaven prosper him! The luckless child would lose

The eyes out of his head and hardly miss.

Ah! yes, good mother (*to* MADAME BOUCHER, *enter-*
    ing), help us. Pray you brace

The sword-belt. O dear sword (*kissing it*), to-day,
    to-day,

You shall not do the deed, but you shall see it.
O me, how tarries Louis with Rolande.

    MADAME BOUCHER.   Dear heart, what heat is this?
        There came no word
To make you arm.

    JOAN.   No word! My Council sent
Word of a fight this moment.

    MADAME BOUCHER.   Ay, and where?

    JOAN.   That is it I'd give my second horse to know.
'Tis haply Fastolfe's succours marching on us,
Or else their forts are stirring.

    MADAME BOUCHER.   Ope me there
A lattice, Marguerite. Yes, be sure, a shout.

    JOAN. O where, then?

    MADAME BOUCHER. From the gate of Burgundy.

    JOAN. It is St. Loup. Away, away!
               (*Runs out and down the stairs.*)

    MADAME BOUCHER.   O child,
She goes to death. Run to her, bid her wait.

    MARGUERITE. I dare not that. O shield her,
        tender God!

    JOAN (*without*). Stand ho! Rolande. Wilt
        make me tarry, thou?

    MARGUERITE (*looking out of window*). Ah! she
        is gone. . . . Nay, what? She turns again.

    JOAN (*without*). The Banner! 'Tis I, my Louis,
        'tis I forget;

I'll never blame you more.   Run, bring it down.
No, reach it to me from the window.

                           Soft,

Good horse, less speed were ours without it: so.
Friend, could you start with me and this forgot?

        LOUIS *enters the room, finds the banner, and reaches*
             it through the window to JOAN

Thanks, Louis, I have it.   Dear my friends, farewell.
   MARGUERITE (*to* LOUIS).   Boy, art thou mazed?
      To horse and after her.   (*Exit* LOUIS.)
   MADAME BOUCHER.   Child,
Keep eye upon her: mine's aswim for fear.
   MARGUERITE.   Hey! but she rides it hotly.   Hold
      your feet,
Rolande, upon the flints.   To see the sparks
Fly from him!   There: she's gone.   Heaven bring
      her back!
   MADAME BOUCHER.   Ay, for the wonderfullest
      soul alive,
And sweetest too.   Come get we to the church,
And pray.   'Tis all we other women can.   (*Exeunt.*)

SCENE VI.—Before the Tourelles. A Fort
of the English at their end of the Bridge

The point of dawn. D'Aulon *with French soldiers
lying under a bank, over which the Tourelles are
seen at a short distance.*

JACQUES.   Is she not coming, sir?   There's blink
of dawn.

D'AULON.   Patience, good fellows, would she fail
the tryst?

JACQUES.   But I'd have at them while the cold's
about,
And they be numb with sleeping.

D'AULON.   Look, she comes.

Enter RAIMOND *and* LOUIS

You, sirs, and not the Maid!

RAIMOND.   We come to learn
If all be here.   She prays till battle-brink,
A field-breadth off, with Pasqucrcl, in the trees.

D'AULON.   We'll need her prayer—five hundred,
spear and bow,
Atop of yonder tower; stark fighters all;
How else? with neck in noose, no doorway out.

They did not think to see French faces, sir,
This side their bridge-head.

  LOUIS.   Is it true she said
She would be hurt to-day?

  D'AULON.   Why, boy, she said it.
Ah! yes: to-day. God send she did but dream,
Like other women.

  SCOT (*rising*). Sir, with reverence,
There's other sight than eyesight. If she saw,
'Twill be.

  D'AULON. Yet cover her, bowman, all you may,
When she sets ladder.

  SCOT.   Troth, all *we* may, sir.
One's yonder steers all arrows, to or fro.
Yet he that hits her—(*goes up stage*).

  RAIMOND.   Honest heart! Would go
World over to pay back the man his bolt.

  D'AULON. Time is one go to warn the Maid.
    Dunois
Has signalled on the right.

  RAIMOND.   Go, Louis, then.
          (*Exit* LOUIS.)
Mayst hear those aspens pattering where she waits.

  D'AULON. The breeze of daybreak.

  RAIMOND.   Ay. Didst hear it said,
Her voice comes clearest when the woods are blown?
Ah! to know now what saith it!

D'AULON.　　　　　　　　　Who was he—
Some saint, but was a fighter—and he kept
His men from onset till he heard the wind
Make sound of going in the tree-top—Hist!
Stand to your arms.　She comes.　(*Aside*) How
　　beautiful
This tender, white girl-wonder foots the brink
Of murder's hellish uproar.　Hark, she speaks.

　　　　　　　(JOAN *appears, mounted.　She beckons the*
　　　　　　　men.)

　　JOAN.　Countrymen, in God's name I lead you.
　　　　Twice
The Maid has led: and God has spoken twice.
Soldiers, we drove them on Ascension eve:
We drove them from St. Laurent yesterday:
And we will drive them from the bridge to-day.
Follow me once again, and France is free.

　　SOLDIERS.　France and the Maid, France and the
　　　　Maid!　Lead on.

　　　　　　　　(*She dismounts and comes forward.*)

　　JOAN.　Yea, will I lead.　With sword I may not
　　　　strike,
Yet strike I will the first blow on their wall.
Give me the ladder.　　　　　　(*They bring it.*)
　　　　　　　　　Friends, the boy that climbs
Quicker than I to rob yon orchard-close,
Will be the nimblest here.　(*Applause of* SOLDIERS.)

My loving Louis,
I cannot risk you yet.   Take you Rolande,
And see you keep him from their arrow flight
Safe in the fence of vineyard : mark me, safe.
How else shall I ride home across the bridge,
A Godon Captain at his bridle-rein ?

LOUIS.   Nay, Maid, beseech you—

JOAN.   Boy, the word is said.
Be knight-like and obey.   (LOUIS *kisses her hand.*)
                              You, Raimond, guard
My banner's bearer.   (*To the bearer*) Shake the
          folds aloft :
High : raise it higher.   (*The sun rises and catches it.*)
                      O Christ, the beam of day
Has lit of all things first our sign that saves.
We conquer, ho ! we conquer.   D'Aulon, bid
Our onset trumpet answer it. . . . On, set on :
Follow me.   God for France and France for God !

          (*Trumpet.   Discharge of ordnance, and
          shouting.   JOAN, followed by soldiers,
          goes up the bank and over it towards
          the Tourelles.*)

SCENE VII.—A Meadow near the Tourelles

Distant shouting and alarums. JOAN *is carried in
    wounded, an arrow sticking in her shoulder,
    by* RAIMOND, JACQUES, *the* SCOT, *and* LOUIS.
    MINSTREL *follows.*

JOAN. Ah! gently; pray you, gentlier.   Every
        step
The arrow stabs.   O I am sore ashamed
Because I cannot hold my tears.   Alack,
I prove but an ill soldier.
        RAIMOND.   Maid, we all
Vow you a miracle of constancy,
Even as of utter daring.
        JOAN.   Ah! no, no.
I am all groans and frailty, being hurt.
        JACQUES.   Why, madam, you do well, I warrant it,
To let the tears run.   It's a helping way.
When I was hurt, good lack! I lay and cursed
The man that hit me (but I make too bold,
Seeing you never let poor soldiers swear).
How so, it eased me wondrous.   And I say,
What cursing is to men be tears to maids.
        RAIMOND.   Peace, Jacques : too free.
        JOAN.   No, let him talk, brave heart.

He fenced me with his body bearing me.

. . . But, oh! to draw this arrow . . . .

RAIMOND. There's no leech
Afield. I would I had the craft of it.

SCOT. Sir, it is best the lady pull it herself:
'Tis safest. Here be oil and bandage.

JACQUES. Hold!
How ye be ignorant all, then! Draw the point
Before ye've charmed . the wound! Why, lack-a-
day,
Wouldst be her death by bleeding? And, by
grace,
There's the mad singer dawdling after us,
Whate'er *he* risk his bones for. He's the sort
That charm the fastest. Say you, fellow there,
Put your crazed wits to purpose : sing's a rhyme
That's good for blood-flow.

JOAN. No, dear God, not that.
Let them not, Raimond. I would rather die
Than salve it with a charm—a devil's aid.

JACQUES. Now say not. Master Rhymer, tell
her you
How charms be sovereign for a bursten vein.
What, man. Dost shake thy head?

MINSTREL. The arrow, the arrow.
The Maid hath power of the arrow (said I not?),
She is too holy to work charms upon.

JACQUES.   Then, ods my life! it's France will
    bleed to death.

You, sir (*to* RAIMOND), persuade her.

JOAN.   No, that shall ye not.
I will not use it, though I died for lack.
Good Louis, bring the Father, if you may,
To hear my shrift.   (LOUIS *goes.*)   And raise me,
    Raimond: so.
Now will I venture.   Stay me, Jesu, stay:
For O to perish, with the deed undone.
Suffer it not: for I will venture. . . . Ah!

                  (*Draws the arrow.*)

Help, for I swoon. . . . (*Falls back, supported by*
    RAIMOND *and* MINSTREL, *who tend the wound.*)

JACQUES (*who picks up the arrow and takes the*
    SCOT *aside*).   Didst mark the Godon, Scot,
    that sent her this?

SCOT.   Ay.

JACQUES.   And couldst know him presently?

SCOT.   Ay.

JACQUES.   And how?

SCOT.   Yon with the slitten cheek, my mark
    belike,
At—how ye call it?—at the Herring-Fight.
We made good shooting, till the centre ran.
I'll clap the next one half-a-handbreadth more
Within the gold.

JACQUES.   So shall ye.   Look ye now.

                              (*Shows the arrow.*)

Here's blood enough upon it.   Touch your points—
Quick, for it dries so fast—and feathers too.
A certain charm to find the smiter.

SCOT.   Man,

Have blood enough o' my own, and fierce enough
To find the smiter.   Let thy charms alone.
Besides, how can ye charm with blood so pure?
Nay, Jacques, I'll none but honest bowcraft.   Back
Both of us to the battle.   Where's the use
To bide?   She's tended well.

JACQUES.   Have with you, Scot.

                              (*They are going.*)

JOAN.   Jacques.

JACQUES.   At your pleasure.

JOAN.   I have work for thee,

When I am back again.

JACQUES.   Command me, Maid.

(*Aside*) If I get through to-day—and she : for how
She pales !   Well, God-a-mercy—

            To PASQUEREL, *entering*

                         Save you, sir :

You're welcome yonder.   (*Exit.*)

PASQUEREL.   Woe is me, dear child,

To see you thus.

JOAN. Nay, now: the worst is o'er.
I am all peace: I think I shall not die.
Yet, sweet my Father, pray for me awhile.
But, first, how do they yonder?

PASQUEREL. There's a pause.
They'd breathe the men, I think, and to it again.

JOAN. Dear Jesu, give them heart to bear it out!
I should be back, Father, I should be back.

PASQUEREL. Nay, daughter, nay: not thus. It
cannot be.
Better you healed than twenty thousand men
And half a year of fighting. Think not of it.
Think of your soul.

JOAN. So will I, yet I know
God does not ask it of me yet. O see,
Dunois.

Enter DUNOIS

How fare we?

DUNOIS. Well—or well enough.
Maid, I am sad for this. How fares the hurt?

JOAN. Bravely. But ask not. Said you 'well
enough'?
But that is *not* well. Stormed ye yet again?

DUNOIS. Once: twice. They piked us from the
copingstone
That last—so near we came. But Glassidas, he,

Roaring to dumb the mortal clamour, ran,
Caught by the wrist one, by the beard one, hurled
Wide of the rampart, swept three ladderheads up
On to his big breast in a sheaf, and tossed
Like sheaf from waggon to the fortalice foot.
'Never I saw such fighting, even in them.
Truth, they are half a thousand boars at bay :
And my poor dogs lie mangled many a one,
And all are faint with harry.   Let it be.
We'll win the top to-morrow.

    JOAN.   No.   To-night.

    DUNOIS.   Why, Joan, you know not.   We are
        spent, I say ;
While they are strangely couraged at your fall,
And stiff as ere you countered them.

    JOAN.   And I
Say, we shall climb to the Tourelles to-night.
Are they so couraged at my fall ?   O then
How will they quail again to see me risen.
For rise I will and back to it.   (*Sits up.*)

    RAIMOND.   Have a heed,
Maid, lest you start the blood.

    DUNOIS.   And, noble Maid,
Be not so absolute and sore in haste.
Yours am I for all service of our war :
Yet, even with you, must I make war by times,
Chances, and means : I tell you, they are spent,

Fitter for sleep than fighting; arm and leg
Sleep of themselves for toil.   It cannot be.

JOAN.   And I tell you, it can be and it shall.
Sir, we will never quarrel, you and I.
Wise are you, wise almost as valorous :
But there's a wisdom, too, of babes, a wit
Shrewder than all you captains of the war,
That ponders not, but only hears and does.
And it is spoken in my heart that God
Will free fair Orleans, and to-day.   But come,
Are your good fellows weary?   Let them sleep :
Two hours or three.   You too.   The captain's head
Is wearier than any fighter's limb.
That made you doubt.   But eat and sleep and rise.
I lead you home, and by the bridge, to-night.

DUNOIS.   I cannot tell why I obey you so,
But I am somehow borne beyond myself
When Joan is speaking, and I trample then
My own good wisdom down, and joy to do it :
And joy to hazard all of mine, and all
The weight of France, to ride the breathless leap
Upon your glorious folly.   Have your way,
Though all we die for it.

JOAN.   Ye shall not die.
Yet must ye feed and sleep before we win.

SCENE VIII.—On the Ramparts of the English Fort at the Bridge-Head

English soldiers (DAKYN, THORPE, ALLERBY, *and* RANDAL) *sitting.* GLANSDALE, *the Captain, enters.*

GLANSDALE. Rest ye now, lads: that was the hottest. Take a bite and drink to wipe your eyes clean, and make better shooting next time. (*Goes off.*)

DAKYN. Ay, mates, here's a sup in comfort at last. They'll not be knocking at our door again yet a while: we slammed it a bit too sharply on their noses that last time.

THORPE. 'Swounds! they pushed smartly: got one foot, as a man may say, 'twixt door and door-post. A shrewd pinch, comrades.

DAKYN. It's they got it, then, for the door went to on 'em.

ALLERBY. Here's to Glansdale that shut it. The company was grown something unhandy till he shook our wits together. What a voice 'a has. It is two parts in seven of a fighting man.

RANDAL. Lord! when he roared at seeing their chins over the top, seemed me as it tore the tower up by the roots, and shook 'em off, and dumped it down on 'em.

F

DAKYN. Wast a bit giddy perhaps, boy, with staring over doom-pit's edge. Beest young at it. Take another cup to settle thy stomach. We'll never look over it so near again.

THORPE. No, they'll be easier driving now she's away; more thanks to Brown Robin that made the hole in her. Why could none of us do it sooner?

ALLERBY. She has done a charm on the bow-strings; they won't carry as they did. But we are all out of gear together for fighting ever since she came among them. It will be the tune of 'George and Merry England' again, now the devil has got his own.

THORPE. Has he? I wish mad Geoffrey had been beforehand with him, when he shinned down the rope to grip her. The madcap truly! How should he bring her in up the wall, saving she was minded to fly?

DAKYN. Tut! Mad Geoff was sane that once; he did not play that for nothing. Had he brought her in, he'd have died esquire, with two hundred crowns to his rent-roll. Lord! 'twould have made a merry burning.

ALLERBY. She'll burn somewhere else fast enough, with Robin's cloth-yard so far through her. A merry life and a short has a witch.

RANDAL. How know we she is witch? She is pleasant-favoured enough.

ALLERBY.   Think'st the devil has no eyes?

RANDAL.   What's that to it?

ALLERBY.   Why, be not witches the devil's wenches?   Then will Satan, like his neighbours, choose a wench by her looks.

THORPE.   Then, Tom, if the devil have eyes, he mostly doesn't use them.   For what say you to old Kate o' the Beard for looks—her that we burnt at Upton Cross?

ALLERBY.   There's a puzzle, out of doubt.   Belike he took *her* for the beauty of her soul, as parson has it, by the rule of contrary.

RANDAL.   Mates, laugh at me if you will, but yon girl's black hair made me think of a lass in Kent I know of.

DAKYN.   Beest a soft-heart, lad.   But your lass won't lie awake to-night for jealousy.   She yonder is sped by now.   So one cup more for——

THORPE.   Ugh!

DAKYN.   What mak'st faces at?

THORPE.   Look! (*points to French post*).

DAKYN.   Hell and—! she's back, and on her feet too!

ALLERBY.   Art sure?

DAKYN.   It were worth twenty crown to us that I were drunk and seeing crooked.   But she's there.

ALLERBY.   Then are we lost sinners all of us.   If

she wriggled.off Rob's skewer sound, she's no devil's wench, but the very devil's own mortal self.

DAKYN. Devil have you, Tom, for talking that way to shake the youngsters. Buckle on your wrist-guard, and don't be a fool. Hasn't arrows a plenty still? If she come again we'll feather her all over, till the witch takes to flying willy-nilly. To your posts, all of you. (*Aside*) Now would I give the five-acre to be back on my farm.

SCENE IX.—A FRENCH POST NEAR THE TOURELLES. PART OF THE BRIDGE IS VISIBLE

Groups of soldiers resting. JOAN *enters*

JACQUES (*rising*). The Maid! A welcome, com-
    rades, to the Maid!
SOLDIERS. Life to the Maid! Long live the weal
    of France!
JOAN. Friends, have ye slept a se'nnight since I
    went,
To make you look so freshly? Ye shall sleep
Another se'nnight presently, if ye will;
For we'll go home to it on the foeman's bridge.
    JACQUES. We've half a year of slumber in the
    head,

But we'll not wink an eye if feats there be
To please the Maid.

JOAN.   Why, Jacques, a feat there is
All for yourself.

JACQUES.   My life on it, 'tis done.

JOAN.   Your life *is* on it.   Take my banner you,
For he that bore is lamed, and he that bears
Will need go far this even.   When we storm,
Keep with the foremost at the fosse-edge, plant
The banner nighest to the wall, and watch
Until the good wind bear it.   If it touch,
We have them.

JACQUES.   Maid, if bones of mine will hold
So long together, I'll do it.

JOAN.   Keep you Heaven !
Here's Father Pasquerel; let him shrive you first,
And who else fights unshriven.   (*To the* CANNONEER)
            Master Jean,
You make good shooting, but you time it ill.

JEAN.   Then thou amend old Jean.

JOAN.   Why thus it is.
Let loose your volley when we sound the rush ;
Then hold: but, when the ladders grip the wall,
Lay old Astounder's muzzle on the hole
That gaps their ramp (they set their stoutest there),
And, first foot upon rungs, touch tinder.   O
To think I send poor souls before their God

Shriftless and in their heat! Not mine the blame:
So oft I warned them hence.

JEAN. And soothly, Maid,
They met your courtesy most uncourteous-wise.
But, howsoe'er, it's kill or else be killed
In war-time, so I'll lay Astounder true.
Let them not climb too fast though, for at whiles
She's slow of speech and stammers.

JOAN. See you keep
The drier priming.

Enter the MARSHALS

Ah! La Hire, Dunois,
Xaintrailles, ye need me. (*They go apart.*) What
        has fallen new?

DUNOIS. Maid, I was idle-bold, and I repent.
We cannot hazard it to-night: the dark
Would catch us ere we end it.

XAINTRAILLES. Were the men
Fresh out of stall, yet are we scant of force.
There's no way in except by storm on storm
With new and new, to wear the tough dogs out.

LA HIRE. I am not qualmish; I can see blood
        flow.
But, Heavens! to see my sturdy fellows mauled,
And all for nothing— Look, in honour of you,

I've loosed not one good curse a fortnight long,
But only fancy oaths and fooleries—.   Maid,
I could not look on that and hold me in.

    DUNOIS.   La Hire is chafed and blunt : forgive
       him it.
But, truth, we have not time or means to fight.

    JOAN.   I see ye have been in council.   So have I.
And yours has reasoned well.   So has not mine.
My Council reason not ; they know, they bid,
Being holy. . . . In God's name, set on to-night.

    DUNOIS.   How shall I say it?   I am chief in trust
Of the King's army.   If I wreck it here
From faith in you, that clears not : I am shamed.
Small matter.   But yourself—.   For mark what hangs.
Let them but win one fight of us, and straight
Our new-wrought spell of prowess crumbles back :
All's to begin, and with twice-broken hearts.
Now dare ye take on you the burden ?

    JOAN (*after a moment's pause*).   Sirs,
Ye urge me very sore, and wise are ye ;
But yet I am not daunted : only now
While you are talking something clouds my mind,
Like wind that ruffles up a glassing pool.
I shall see clearly, were I once alone.
I do not think to change : yet suffer me
One short half-quarter of an hour apart
In yonder applegarth.

DUNOIS.   So be it, Maid.

                                  (JOAN *goes.*)

The MINSTREL *sings*

From the noise of archers in the place of drawing
    water,
    From the lightnings of the quiver,
From the bitter leaguer and the hunger and the
    slaughter,
    Is there helper, is there any,
    Is there any can deliver?
        Nay, is none.
    Be the sons of France so few,
    Be her men too weak to do,
    Be the lords of her untrue?
    No, their ranks are stout enow:
    No, their sword is sharp, I trow:
O but God, who mad'st them many,
        Make them one!

Who is this alighted from the skirts of skyland hither,
    All in sunlight for an armour,
White dove wings a-hover in the banner blowing with
    her:
    And aneath her, blunted wholly,
    Lies the arrow that would harm her,
        Undertrod?
    O by sign of snows and fire,

O by whispers that aspire
Of a heaven-wind stooping nigher,
Follow, France, the banner's breath,
Follow down the pass of death,
France, the dove-flight of the holy
Maid of God.

JOAN *re-enters*

MINSTREL. Behold!
D'AULON. Can this be war? She comes so still.
RAIMOND. Her eye's all battle : she has seen
Them there.
JOAN. Dunois, my Council met me in the trees.
Dunois, they bade us in the name of God
Set on, and conquer.
DUNOIS. Yea, He wills, He wills.
Heaven and the Maid for France!
JOAN. Array the storm.
This time I lead not. I am bidden abide
And overlook the fight, not mingle in it.
I will stand still and see what God will do.

There must be one beside me for a need :
Stay, Raimond. Father, go not back, for we
Must pray the more, not fighting. (*To the* SOLDIERS)
Soldiers all,

Hearken.   I send my banner to the fort,
Alone : but with it march the Holy Ones.
Fasten your eyes upon it.   If it touch
Yon wall, we have them.

> SOLDIERS *shout.*   France and Holy Maid !
> JOAN.   One word, Dunois.   (*They talk.*)
> D'AULON (*to* JACQUES).   Basque, dost thou keep
>   the flag ?
> JACQUES.   Yes, while I keep my hands, sir.
> D'AULON.   Look on me.

When fights are won, they're won by two or three,
Not many.   Here is one.   Wilt be the other ?

> JACQUES.   God and the Maid so help me.
> D'AULON.   See, 'tis sworn.

When I leap in the ditch, come after you.
The banner shall touch wall.

> JACQUES.   'Tis sworn.   Away.

>   (*Exeunt with* DUNOIS *and* SOLDIERS.
>   JOAN,   RAIMOND, *and* PASQUEREL
>   *remain.*)

> JOAN.   Hence can we see them.
> RAIMOND.   Why so near ?   Their shot

Can strike you.

> JOAN.   If it come but hitherward.

It will not come.   O Raimond, we shall win :
Shall win. . . . Why does La Hire so linger ? he
That is such hot-foot else.

RAIMOND.   He spreads his men
Better to lap their bastion.

JOAN.   We shall win.
They told me we shall win it. Raimond, friend,
Girl am I yet, as when you knew me first,
And dreadful is this silence. Help me, Christ !
I know we cannot fail. But O, to stand
Here on the shivering precipice edge and watch
The world swing under us. Help me, friend : your
    hand,
Dear Raimond. . . . Ah ! the live and steady
    clasp !
A moment back I seemed a ghost : and now—

    RAIMOND. Your hand is cold with travail of heart,
    and yet
It sends a fire across me. Maid, I know,
I too, that we shall win.

JOAN.   O Lord, how long ?
Take you this other hand, sweet Father : take,—
Pray that Joan faint not.

    RAIMOND (*looking across river*). That is strange, .
    I vow.

    PASQUEREL. What see you ?

    RAIMOND.   Musters on the townward side,
That thicken at the bridge-head—what to do ?
The bridge is gapped ; they cannot cross to
    help.

PASQUEREL.　They do but watch us.　Mark the
　　Maid, how rapt.
She heeds not.

JOAN.　　　　　' Voices, voices . . . heard we true ?
Voice in the woodland. . . . Nay, my heart, 'tis
　　so.'

PASQUEREL.　What does she murmur ?

RAIMOND.　　　　　　　　God ! 'twas this she sang
Once in the meadow.　' Voices.'　Make them true,
O God of truth ; betray not. . . . Father, look :
A miracle ! they have flung a bridge in air,
And spanned yon arches.　'Tis a plank, no more.
Yet there goes one upon it.　O brave foot,
Heaven steady it : and another——— (*A bugle sounds.*)
　　　　　　　　　　　　　　　Joan, awake.
They peal the onset.

JOAN.　　　　　　　Loose me, loose.　O sword,
　　　(*Plucks her hands away and holds her
　　　sword before her by the blade.*)
O Sword my Cross, be sword and cross to-day :
Smite them, deliver us. (*Alarums.*)　Goes the banner
　　first ?

RAIMOND.　Ay, with a bolt stuck fast in't.　Ah !
　　he's hit.
'Tis nought : he plunges on : he's first at fosse.

JOAN.　They spake me truth : They will not fail me.

RAIMOND.　　　　　　　　　　　　　　See,

D'Aulon has leaped. O follow him, follow. . . . Alas,
Has it fallen?

JOAN.   O my banner, God on high!
My banner!

RAIMOND.   No, it rises. 'Twas the Basque
Sprang to the ditch. He rears and shakes it out.

JOAN.   Watch, watch!   O carry it, Wind of
        God!

RAIMOND.   It touched. . . .
Roar, France, and leap the rampart! Up, up, up!
They climb with wings, not ladders. 'Tis a flight
Of birds that swarm to a tree-top. . . . Roar again,
France! we have swept them from the battlements:
There's not a foeman upright in the fence.
God, Thou hast heard her!

JOAN (*to herself*).   They were true, were true.

RAIMOND (*hastily*).   Hear me, while I can speak
        it.   There's an awe
Come on me and a shame.   I know thee now:
God's angel more than woman.   Holy Maid,
If ever this unknowing heart that loves
Loved thee not as the thing thou art, forgive.
I kiss thy hand, fair angel: I am taught.
O me unworthy!

JOAN.   Raimond, what is this?
I can but half conceive you; but I know
Your words are strange, and trouble the great joy.

And, look, it is not done. There's fighting yet
Round the Tourelles,—how comes it ?—from the town.

    PASQUEREL. Saw you not how the townsmen cast
      the plank,
To storm upon the counter-side ? And see,
There's Glassidas makes at them o'er the bridge,
—Lo ! where he stood to curse you—sword in air,
Rallying his last about him.

    JOAN (*shouting to* GLANSDALE). Madman, yield !
Yield to the King of Heaven ! I pardon thee
That bitter malice. Save thy soul alive,
For God will ask it suddenly— (*Bridge falls.*) O
      he's gone.
Our foes are fallen, are fallen : the floods go o'er,
The floods have swallowed him and swept away,
And all his evil on him. O I could weep
My heart out for the pity of souls of men,
That die so woeful swift. Pardon him yet,
Merciful Powers : he knew not what he said.
Run, Raimond, pluck some drowner from the stream
Ere the mail sink them : quick. What help need I ?
                      (RAIMOND *runs off.*)
My God is all around me like a host.
And where is the oppressor ?

    PASQUEREL.   Maiden, turn :
Dunois would greet you.

    DUNOIS (*entering*).   Nay, no words have I.

My heart is liker fall in tears than words,
So charged with joy and wonder.   France is saved,
And all the deed a woman's.

 JOAN.   Say not so.
God saves by whom He will; give glory there.
Now must we homeward, sir, across the bridge.

 DUNOIS.   Why, Maid, 'tis gone.

 JOAN.   Yet by the bridge will I.
I promised and I'll do.   The nimble wrights
That spanned an arch for battle, shall they not
Span it for triumph?   And I think, Dunois,
A bridge of gossamer were enough to prop
The weight of marching France this happy night:
So light our heart is we could tread the air.

         (*They march off.*)

ACT II

SCENE I.—GARDEN BEFORE THE CASTLE OF LOCHES

Enter RAIMOND, *singing*

Mortal born, and lovest a star,
    White fire all to the heart thereof?
Stars are lone as heaven is wide,
How wilt win thee a star for bride?

      Sooth, my star
      Is afar, too far.
    Yet is it good to love.

Old singer of the Southland, knew you that?
You rhymed it of a simple boy that loved
A star of court too princely throned for him.
Mine is not high, yet higher by all a heaven
Than any star of court, and sevenfold more
Not to be reached than these are, isled away

In virgin airs unbreathable of men.
Is Raimond fool to love the star? a babe
Dancing a palm to pluck a brightness down,
That seems an armlength-sundered jewel, and is
Lamp of unsounded deeps?   O tell me not!
I love and have not, yet to love is good.
And, good or ill, I can no otherwise.
But good it will be.   Star in hopeless height,
I shall not climb the skies, but climb I shall
Nearer the skies by longing for the star,
So am I boldened and so winged by love.
Yea, all things else I covet one are grown
With her, are semblances and hues of her.
She's France to me and fame and golden deed,
And veiled Fair-fortune beckoning wooers on,
And all youth dreams or dares.   But hush, my soul,
For how should love have voice that hath not hope?

Enter GUV DE LAVAL *behind him*

GUV.   Aha! my Raimond.   Stolen away so far?
'Twas churlish on a feast.   Yet, if my ears
Are quick as otherwhiles, I read your hap.
There's a love-ditty making for some fair.
Ay, shake your blushful head : deny it.   Yes,
'Tis so prescribed in books of gallantry.
Well, happy you that find her.   As for me,

G

I am three months at court, and cannot find
Those beauties that were vaunted.   Which is yours
I'll guess anon without one envious pang.

    RAIMOND.   You need no envy, Guy, for fair of
        mine.

Guess on : you will not guess the riddle, friend,
That has no answer.

    GUY.   By and by.   But now
Art thou not wearying till the war is up?

    RAIMOND.   Know'st how it went this morn in
        council?

    GUY.   No.

Not well it went; so cloudy is the Maid.
And yet her spleen becomes her.   Raimond, lad,
I tremble for your fair Unnamed.   'Tis she
Has need of envy, seeing you so close
In favour of the wondrous Maiden.   True,
She's not of us, nor yet for love at all,
Even were she gentle.   Shame ; I bite my tongue
For mingling up her name with railleries.
She is a maid to worship, a thing apart,
Not gentle and not simple, but divine.
I thought her so, and Andrè thought the like,
That time we met her, and she called for wine,
And pledged the day when we should drink with her
In Paris of the French.   'Twas solemn-sweet,
And like a sacring of the blessed Cup.

Yea, yea, divine is she. But who can tell?
'Twere pity if this virgin chase from her
All the true hearts, and then, some altered day,
Fall back to the least worthy. See you, though,
Here's my great cousin coming, deep in talk
With Regnault and De Gaucourt. Let's avoid.

(*They retire.*)

Enter TREMOUILLE, REGNAULT, DE GAUCOURT

TREMOUILLE. Something too soon you yielded at
    the board,
Regnault. You churchmen hearts (all honour!)
    keep
Such welcome for what pleads in name of Heaven.
I call our mystic girl Heaven's gift, and yet
A gift to use, not squander. Follow her on
In too fantastic venture, and you break,
Like the fool-heir who cracked his charmèd glass,
Our talisman of fortune.
    REGNAULT.   Can I waive
My office of God's judge in things of God?
I thought with you: but when her cheek took
    fire,
Telling how came the voice, 'Go on, go on,
Daughter of God,' it rang so golden-true,
I knew it for heaven's mintage and not earth's.

Tremouille. Well, you, not I, are heaven's
   assayer. And yet—
Nay, it is not my province.
   Regnault.   Say it out.
   Tremouille. Then, seems it not this envoy
   spiritual
Is something scant of deference to the sway
Of spiritual Powers ordained? For me,
I think (but you are large and generous,
And in your own cause loth to note affront)
Daughter of God were daughter of the Church.
You preach us, you divines, of carnal pride
Marring fair works. Fear you not this?
   Regnault.   The Church
Is careful of her rule, not jealous. Where
Has Joan so lacked correction?
   Tremouille.   O not that;
No trespass. No; an air, a glance, a pose,
A mood of curbed impatience while you spoke;
No more. But let it pass. You saw it not:
Why vex you with it? More imports how fared
State's policy. Here I turn me from my lord
Archbishop to my lord the Chancellor.
We base on statesmanship : we dread to watch
The tissues of your rare diplomacy,
Ere the fine hand could twine them into cords,
To reive up Duke with King, swept grossly through

By a girl's marshal-baton.   That is why,

Estopped myself by failure of your lead,

I craved more stiffness in our Chancellor.

REGNAULT.   I cannot hold myself to blame.   The
folk

Are passionate for the girl.   De Gaucourt knows

What the man risks who shuts a door on her.

DE GAUCOURT. Stoning in open street, if me you ask.

A pleasant passage and rememberable.

And two-score years a soldier !   Well, the Turks

For me : they're easier foughten than a wench.

REGNAULT.   Even so.   And statesmanship will
strain no power

Save for clear profit.   Give her passion rein,

Then ride and guide.   The purse-strings of the state

Are bridle at need.   And, Tremouille, if she win,

We treat on prouder terms with Burgundy :

If fail, not *we* have failed, our counsel stands

Approved by practice.

TREMOUILLE.   Have it so, my lord.

I am half myself persuaded.

REGNAULT.   Well, the King

Has dined and needs me.   You, De Gaucourt, too ?

DE GAUCOURT.   Ay, spite of wenches, needs the
old soldier still.

We'll go.   Farewell, my lord of Tremouille.

(*Exeunt* REGNAULT *and* DE GAUCOURT.)

Tremouille.　The fox, the ox: a couple strangely
　　yoked
That I must plough with.　Swish your tail, Sir Ox,
You will not scare that gadfly of your spleen
While I can keep it buzzing.　You, Sir Fox,
Regnault—Reynard . . . tut, call him hare, that stole
A fox's hide and airs the brush as proud
As peacock fan, to warrant us his craft.
And lo, the proof!　He has my scheme by heart
(How solemn he rehearsed the lesson now!),
Thinks it his own, will boast it for his own,
Will cradle it, father it,—and be hanged for it,
Poor fox-skin, if it fail us.　Will it fail?
The folk so worship her.　The Maid, the Maid!
So worshipful it seems then to be maid.
What's so divine in maidenhood?　And yet
She beats the English by it, and she beats
In them La Tremouille.　Let her win too long,
And soon my bantling prince will grow the wings
I keep so trimly clipped.　A maid, forsooth!
Why should it be so strong to be a maid?
'Tis somewhat rare, i' faith, as manners are.
. . . Ha! but I have it . . . the holy maidenhood,
Can we not alter that?　For there be ways.
How might our maid be prosperously wife . . .
Or, better, less than wife and more than maid?
That were the master stroke.　Or, least and worst,

Might we entangle her, make rumour's breath
Bedamp this crystal of virginity
With 'Our cold virgin has a heart, a heart
Like all the world.' Yes, yes, some gallant boy,
Hired in my own Poitou, would pleasure me.
I'll bear the costs of marriage—or the attempt,
Or . . . In the name of (which shall I invoke
Justlier at such concurrence?) here's the man
Made for my service.

RAIMOND approaches

Walk you still, young sir?
RAIMOND.   I wait in duty.
TREMOUILLE.   On the Maid?
RAIMOND.   On her.
TREMOUILLE.   A happy service, with your leave
     to say it.
RAIMOND.   My lord, I think it.
TREMOUILLE.   And you march with her
To the new fights on Loire?
RAIMOND.   Most blithe indeed,
—So my commission hold.
TREMOUILLE.   And holds it not?
RAIMOND.   My lord, I thought that rested with
     yourself.
TREMOUILLE.   Nay, doth it so? That it should
     'scape me! Sir,
Forgive it, for my head is thronged of late.

But, since my choice has prospered so, believe
It will not change.

    RAIMOND.   My lord, I thank you well.

    TREMOUILLE.   The thanks are mine to pay. We
        cannot choose

With a too prosperous art her gentlemen,
Our safeguard's own safeguarders.

    RAIMOND.   We shall do
Our manliest in the trust.

    TREMOUILLE.   Yea, do ye that:
And your most prudent too, so much she dares.
I have a qualm at moments how we jar
This costly vessel in our hurtling fights.
'Oft to the fount, at last to wreck,' is said
Of common clays. Prove it not true of hers!
Yet she must fear it, for she tells the King
Her 'time is short.' Sir, have you light on this?

    RAIMOND. None. But she bade him use her
        while he may.

That speaks not fear.

    TREMOUILLE.   Why, no: you read her well.
You have her mind, if any. But I would find
A gentle reading. She will end the war
As swiftly as triumphantly, ungird
Her harness, and be wed by some—

    RAIMOND.   My lord,
She will not wed.

TREMOUILLE.   O then you know it?

RAIMOND.   I?

'Tis common knowledge.   'Maiden' is her name.

TREMOUILLE.   For use in camps, I take it.   War
      at end,

Why weds she not as all?

RAIMOND.   I cannot say.

And yet she will not.

TREMOUILLE.   More's the pity then.

A noble bride: I'll say it, a noble's bride;

Her birth not hindering.   Sooth, it rather steads:

Who breaks that bar will be the generous heart,

The deeper-seeing, and that loves for worth.

There are such, yes, in our hard days.   Besides

Kings can ennoble at will.   But, out on us!

We gossip like old damozels; I to blame.

The rest is earnest.   Sir, there must be one

Whom the Maid trusts, and whom the King may trust,

To eye her weal in his more special name.

He is most jealous for her.   In the wars

Are other soldiers than a foe's to dread

For Joan.   Her nearest in regard are you

(Nay, for we know it); use your nearness well,

Lest others near her; like a friend, beset:

And, as you may, keep level with her thought,

That she may trust one loyal gentleman

With hint of danger if she see it, and we,

Warned by yourself, give succour. Enough. You
    hear
And understand. I see the King thereon.
Wait not his word; your warrant is my own.
But he forgets not, sir, what men are true,
And secret, in his cause.

    RAIMOND.   My lord, the task
For the King's warrant is more sacred still.
Unwarranted, I had laid it on my faith.

    TREMOUILLE.   Even so. But now the King has
    laid it there;
He looks to you. Give you good even, sir.

    RAIMOND. And you, my lord.   (*Goes up stage.*)

    TREMOUILLE (*looking after him*). I have lodged
    the philtre in him:
 . . . If he but love her as I hate her—'Sdeath!
There'll be hot wooing.   (*Goes.*)

    RAIMOND (*turning and coming forward*). What to
    think of this?
Is he so false then? False or true, the charge
Is pure: the King's word sweetly chimes with love's.
Something he shadowed of advancement. Heart,
Forget it: love shall work for love. And still
How jumps it with my fancy, that the Maid
Was France to me, and fame, and golden deed.
'Tis Fortune beckoning from the gates of Love
To one same path. And then, 'her time is short.'

Come, Peace, and change her.   O in one quick hour
How much more near the mortal stoops the star !

(Goes.)

SCENE II.—A Hall in the Castle of Loches

Marguerite *and* Raimond

Marguerite.   So you must go to-morrow, Guy
   and you,
To help Joan drive the English.
   Raimond.   As we mean.
   Marguerite.   Take care then of her.
   Raimond.   Care ?   How should I not ?
   Marguerite.   Not too much, neither.   ˌ
   Raimond.   And how should I that ?
   Marguerite.   Well, well.   How can I say ?   But
   you are wise.
'Tis true : for two nights since La Tremouille
Told me himself.
   Raimond.   And, damsel, was he right ?
   Marguerite.   I might have known to answer
   weeks ago.
Now—why, we talk but seldom.
   Raimond.   Am I fallen
Of late from better manners ?   Yet, methinks,
Your kindness brings you, where my duty me,
To the Maid's side, not seldom.

MARGUERITE.   Do you think
La Tremouille was so right to call you wise?

RAIMOND.   You said it, and not I.

MARGUERITE.   La Tremouille
Trusts you in much.   Oh, but he told myself!

RAIMOND.   Why, then, belike he does.

MARGUERITE.   In gratitude,
You should return it, should you not?

RAIMOND.   What, I?
The Squire to him the Councillor?   But I see
You trifle.

MARGUERITE.   Ah, sir, no. . . . La Tremouille
Speaks very honourable things of Joan.

RAIMOND.   Why, can he help himself?

MARGUERITE.   La Tremouille
Is very careful for her.

RAIMOND (*angrily*).   What is this?
Tremouille, Tremouille, Tremouille.   Is there one
Name only we can talk of?

MARGUERITE.   O the heat!
And I so thought the theme would pleasure you!

RAIMOND.   You mean some mischief, though I
          guess not what.

MARGUERITE.   There may be mischief, and *I* guess
          not what.
Let's talk of other things.   My lord—of Sully
(Since my lord's proper name enrages you)—

Is provident for Joan.   (*Pauses.*)

                                    A yeoman's wife
Upon our lands would lie awake at nights,
For tender care about a steer, but she,
Good soul, was thinking upon Martinmas
And saltings against Yule.   O how my tongue
Runs off to trifles!   See!   I prove you right.

    RAIMOND.   Will you not tell me, damsel, what
        you mean?

    MARGUERITE.   When I am meaning nothing?
        And besides
Joan has a proverb, 'Men be hanged at times
For speaking truth.'

    RAIMOND.   Then, damsel, time it is
We risk so much between us, being friends.
I see you hate this lord we speak of.

    MARGUERITE.   Hate?
O sir, what have I said but in his praise?

    RAIMOND.   You do him wrong to praise, and
        wrong to hate;
I wrong him neither way, but hold he seeks
Joan's welfare, not as we for love, and yet
Truly, from sober reckoning of the gain.
I grant he has no fervour for her faith;
But he pretends none.   Man of state is he;
Not spiritual, yet approves a spiritual aid,
And out of cold good-counsel does the right.

You women, like the children, write men down
Good, bad: white, black: 'I love,' or 'I detest.'
You cannot take a man for what he is,
And use him.

    MARGUERITE.   Ah! you mean to use the lord
We name not; use!   I had not thought of that.
I' faith, 'tis prettily conceited.

    RAIMOND.   There!
Mocking as ever.

    MARGUERITE.   Mocking! if you knew
How sore my heart is for this Heart of France,
Our wondrous Joan, and how the nameless fear
Creeps, at a someone's shadow passing by!
Oh, sir, you shall not be the death of her!

    RAIMOND.   God's life!   I'd die myself a hundred
        times
For Joan!   You know it.

    MARGUERITE.   Better were to live.

    RAIMOND.   As live I will.   What is it I would
        not do?

    MARGUERITE.   He does not always best who does
        the most,
About a maiden. . . . There's a step I know;
Quick, promise me to guard her with your life,
And never to forget.

    RAIMOND (*kissing her hand*).   Be sure of me.
                     (*Exit* RAIMOND.)

GUY *entering, hears his last words*

GUY (*aside*).   'Be sure of him.'   Why, so, till now,
    was I.
(*Aloud*) Damsel, I came to take my leave.
MARGUERITE.   Your friend
Raimond, and I, were speaking of you now.
    GUY.   *My* friend; not yours then?
MARGUERITE.   Mine, as well you know.
    GUY.   I knew, at least, he was not less than friend.
MARGUERITE.   'Not less than friend.'   It sounds
    a riddle.   Is it?
But do not ask me guess it, for my mind
Is very dull, with thought of losing you—
The twain of you, I mean—besides the Maid.
It will be grim at Court when you are gone.
    GUY.   Would any one of us have served without
The others?
    MARGUERITE.   Better one than none.   And yet,
O fie on me, to choose my company!
There is no Maid like ours, there is no friend
More loyal than is Raimond, and no knight
More gallant than Laval.
    GUY (*aside*).   This tune is sweeter.
I heard amiss.
    MARGUERITE.   Now, could you choose, Sir Guy,
Between them, you, if you were Marguerite?

GUY. Ay,
And easily, for, were I Marguerite,
Then Marguerite were Laval, and I should choose
That gallant knight undoubting.

MARGUERITE. There again
A riddle, and I cannot play the game,
I am so sad at parting. Brave my knight,
Farewell, and fight the battles of the Maid ;
But wisely too the while, and bring her home
Safe, and yourself. One out of three to choose
Is hard : oh, how much harder then to lose.

(Is going, but returns.)
See, here's a feather moulted from my cap.
'Twould fit a steel cap better. Will you try ?

(Gives him a feather and goes.)

SCENE III.—A CHAMBER IN LA TREMOUILLE'S
CASTLE OF SULLY

CHARLES, TREMOUILLE, REGNAULT, LE MAÇON
in council

REGNAULT. One other matter claims your notice,
sire,
The Second Council of the Realm awaits
The royal seal.

CHARLES.   I had forgot.   (*Seals a paper.*)   We
    hope
Much profit, Regnault, of your pains upon it.
TREMOUILLE.   I count this parcelling of the
    kingdom's charge,
Sire, of your happiest thoughts.   My Lord of Rheims,
We owe you for your boldness, who accept
Our perilous North : but then no less we owe
For the tried skill which warrants it.
REGNAULT.   My thanks
To my Lord Dauphin shall be paid in toils.
Le Maçon, have we news yet of the camp
Asking decision ?
LE MAÇON.   News, but vague and crossed.
At Jargeau and at Meun our arms, it seems,
Prosper.   The happier this, because I hear
Of ill content among the chiefs.
TREMOUILLE.   Ah ! so ?
Where should this lie ?
LE MAÇON.   Betwixt the Maid and them.
She bears it with too high a hand, they say,
And brooks no peer in council.
TREMOUILLE.   Gentle sire,
Your chiefs must bear it.   Kings themselves, if envy
Were not too low for them, might feel its prick,
When they are served too well.
CHARLES.   How mean you that ?

TREMOUILLE. That chiefs should take example
    by their prince,
And be magnanimous. You gave her, you,
Absolute trust, who might have doubted well
Lest she who makes the kingdom yours should make
The kingdom's heart her own. You doubted not.
The chiefs must brook her then.

    CHARLES.   We note in her
A reverence steadfast as her service is.

    TREMOUILLE. May wisdom keep it still unspoiled.
    My fear
Were rather of the undiscerning herd,
Men of the ranks that make their songs of her,
Men of the streets that worship. Well, what harm?
If turning Fortune turned their simple head,
The folly passes with the war. I strayed
(My error) from the purpose: may we count
These late successes give us rest?

    LE MAÇON (*who has gone to the door, and returned*).
    My liege,
The Maid's esquire waits at the door, and craves
Audience on her behalf.

    CHARLES.   Admit him.

    RAIMOND *enters and salutes* CHARLES

                         Sir,
You come with news?

RAIMOND.   My liege, the noblest.   France
Has clashed with England's best on open field,
And driven them to the winds.

CHARLES.   Ah ! good is Heaven.
(*Aside*) Then was I heard : then am I king indeed.

 RAIMOND.   And Talbot, the great Talbot's self
  is taken.

 CHARLES.   Why, wonder is outwondered.   More ;
  say more.
Make us believe.

RAIMOND.   My liege, I shall not fail.
How Jargeau fell before us, how the bridge
Of Meun, and how Beaugency, have you heard.
The next shall make you well forget them all.
My lord, when news was brought us how Fastolfe,
Long dreaded, ranged by Talbot's side at last,
Re-forcing him from England, doubts had we
If we might hold our winnings ; but the Maid
Flashed out a 'God be thanked, we have them all :
Look that your spurs be sharp'; and when we stared,
Asking her meaning, 'Sooth, to hunt the fliers !'
So swept us on to battle.   North of Loire,
So tangled is the plain, we feared to spend
A week of Blindman-hunting in the woods.
But from a launde's edge at our feet upsprang
A ten - branched stag, leaping the launde, and
  plunged

Through the far covert rustling : when a sound
Rose to make French blood spring, a foreign cry
Of venery, then an answer, and in a trice
A long *halali* volleying down a line
Of jocund hunters at a quarry's rouse :
And they the launde-breadth off their mortal foes !
Sire, I am French, but half my heart with them
Bounded, at note of the blithe woodsman glee,
To hunt with them, not slay.   But dumb we stayed
Warning the host behind, till fierce La Hire
Upspurring hurled us on them.   Hot we came,
Ere they could crown a rise or plant a stake,
And rolled their archery in an instant wreck
Down on their startled pikes, and swept the twain,
A groaning, helpless welter of huddled arms,
Back, back, and into fragments.   There I saw
Heaving upon the rearward-eddying war
Grim Talbot, with a half-score spears at back,
Wheel his big sorrel, as were't a barque, to ride
The wave down of our horsemen, but the wave
Rode *him* down and went over.   There behind
Came all too late Fastolfe, whom Talbot's wreck,
Flung by our storm upon his ordered front,
Like a dead hulk that, staggering blind across
A seaway, grinds a living galley's side,
Smote on and broke and foundered.   All the
        Beauce

Was strowed with drift of that disaster.   Sire,
There is no host of England left afield :
Not Paris gate could bar us, came you there.

 TREMOUILLE (*aside*).   So fast, sir ! Fool, to let
   her grow to this.

(*Aloud*) My liege, I am lost in glory like yourself.
'No English host afield.'   At last, at last
Rest in your borders !   Thank we all the Maid
Who ends as she began.

 CHARLES.   Not ends, my lord :
There's yet the consecration.   Has not this
Opened our way to Rheims ?

 RAIMOND.   To Rheims ! my King,
To Rheims !   O no, to Paris, to the sea.

 TREMOUILLE.   Your youngest counsellor has the
   speed, my liege,
Of us, who know but the affairs of state.

 CHARLES.   Nay, Tremouille, nay.   What harm ?
   The gallant lad
Brings burning news.   If he be hot withal,
I will not blame him.

 RAIMOND.   Grace, my noble liege,
For my rash speaking.   All the camp is hot
(I did but speak their thought) to bring you
   thither.

 TREMOUILLE.   Ah ! let me not, young sir, be
   taken amiss.

I did but smile to mark your valiant heat
Outrun us tardy men of state.   Indeed,
My royal master, he is wise as hot
In every faithful office, and the Maid,
For so I learn, prizes his counsel well.

    RAIMOND.   No, no; you credit me too far.   The
        Maid
Honours a childish friendship; that is all.

    TREMOUILLE (*to* CHARLES).   Well, not to quarrel
        with his modesty,
I will but say your royal need will find
No surer servant.   For the march to Rheims,
Your chancellor, if I read his looks, will urge
As reason for demur——

    USHER (*entering*).   Your Grace, the Maid
Craves audience.

    CHARLES.   How! So quick?   Her messenger
Has scarce outstripped her.   Let her enter.

    TREMOUILLE.   Sire,
Were it not well before she comes, to hear
The Chancellor tell us——

    CHARLES.   What!. And keep door shut
On her?   Such deed, and such a welcome home!
Admit her straightway.   No, Sir Raimond, you
Leave us not yet.   I would have soldiers know
How we received their leader.

Enter JOAN, *who falls at* KING'S *feet*

Ah, not so.

Joan shall not kneel in such an hour as this.

Daughter of France, in the great name of France

I give thee her salute. (*Kisses her on brow.*)

Alas! no thanks

Of ours can match this wonder.

JOAN. O no, no!

Pray you, no thanks for Joan. I only bade

Your soldiers fight and fear not, and the Lord

Of battles threw the foe. The deed is His.

CHARLES. Yea, Maid, but had He done it without
Joan?

JOAN. O gentle Dauphin, there is nothing done.

CHARLES. Nothing! And you in one miraculous
week

Have broken England.

JOAN. Nothing done, until

The Dauphin is the King. O, you will set

Forward to Rheims to-morrow. (CHARLES *is silent.*)

Dear, my liege,

You cannot doubt me still. . . . O pray you,
speak.

CHARLES. Joan, I will go with you.

(*Glancing at* TREMOUILLE.)

My lords, I say it.

REGNAULT.   It rests but with your Grace to say it.
   And yet—
But shall the Council meet and speak of this?
   CHARLES.   We are in council now.   Speak on,
   my lord.
   REGNAULT.   Since I am bidden.   And in truth
   my drift
Is scarce a secret of your Council.   Sire,
You cannot without soldiers march on Rheims;
And as Le Maçon will report, the chest
Holds not a coin to pay them.
   CHARLES.   Is it so?
Maid, I had thought——
   JOAN.   O sire, what hinders it?
Upon my faith, you shall not need a coin
To pay your soldiers; they will fight unfee'd
With merry heart, to have you crowned at Rheims.
A hundred ancient gentlemen of France
(And ask Sir Raimond here to witness me)
Would sell their fathers' acres, the good horse
Between their knees, the gay coat off their back,
And tramp afoot like yeomen at your side
To see your sacring-hour.   Away, away.
God wills it.
   TREMOUILLE (*aside*).   'Sdeath, the girl is glorious.
Can one be foiled and love the child that foils?
Ah!

CHARLES.   Sire de Tremouille, were you speaking?

TREMOUILLE.   No.

This ardour of our maiden general

So much o'ercomes me.   Then, her counsel is

Warranted by such deeds.   I am ashamed

To follow her with cold reasons.   Must I speak?

CHARLES.   We wait your mind.

TREMOUILLE.   My own it is not.   I

Think Regnault leaves unurged an interest

He guards in chief.   He is treating (do I break,

So far, a Council secret?) with the Duke.

Regnault must more instruct us, but I fear,

Greatly I fear, lest by too much parade

Of our new prowess (Maid, our thanks for it!)

We flutter-off the alliance.   Philip gives

More than we claim : but he must give it, not

Unhand it as to force.   Leave him to weigh

The silent eloquence of our Maiden's deeds :

It will incline him more to render grace,

While there's an hour for grace.   Once trumpet out

Our menace to the foes of France, and he

Draws in affronted, bids us snatch by arms,

If so we prosper, what had else been ours

Bloodless, and with his friendship.   I have spoken.

REGNAULT.   And weightily.   What say ye, Joan,
        to this?

JOAN.   I say my lord has bidden go to Rheims.

REGNAULT. 'My lord'?   I understand you not.
   The King?

JOAN.   Ah, yes, the King of Heaven, our Dauphin's
   King.
He never said one word of Burgundy :
He said but only 'Go to Rheims, and crown
The Dauphin King.'   He spoke it plain.   Then what,
Sirs, is there left?

TREMOUILLE.   She will not understand.
Joan, when men asked you once what need there was
Of soldiers, if God willed that France be saved,
You answered, ' Let the soldiers fight, and God
Will make them conquer.'   So I answer now,
' Let statesmen treat, God make the treaty sure.'

JOAN.   He never speaks of treaties.   He has said,
' Be crowned at Rheims.'

TREMOUILLE.   Surely : but in good hour.
For does the sacring press?   Your Grace is King
(This Maid be thanked) in what of power is real.
The form, the holy ritual, of our folk
So prized, is not to be foregone : and yet
Shall we risk substance for a show?

JOAN.   A show !
The high God's own anointing of His own ;
The grace that makes a prince to rule, a folk
Obey him !   No, but I misheard it : you
Cannot think this wise of the holy thing.

I know you are Councillor of State, I know
You have to judge of means and times and men,
Of things how far beyond my knowing, yet,
O my good lord, God has a book whereon
You that are learned and I the simple can
Read at each other's side together.   Sir,
We know you seek but to advance the state
By the wise mind Heaven gave you; then be
    you
Not angry that a girl, who never learnt
To write a word or read a mortal book,
Has asked you to come read this page with her,
And put your wisdom all away.   My lord,
You have to mingle always with the world,
And hear its voices, and attend its work,
O but in your good heart I verily think
You too can hear the voice, and see the hand
That beckons, as I hear it, and I see.   (*Pauses.*)
No?   (*To* REGNAULT) Help him, you that have the
    charge for Christ.
            (*Looks from the one to the other, then turns
                to* CHARLES.)
Sire, it is God's will, if they see it or no.
He will fulfil it.   And yet——

   CHARLES.   What is it, Joan?
What is this 'yet' of yours?

   JOAN.   Nay, pardon me.

CHARLES. But you must tell me, Joan. I saw
    your face
Change, and a trouble cross it. Speak it then.

JOAN. Something remembered out of childish days,
How I heard said, 'God's promise never fails,
But if men fail to wish for it.' And now
It struck me cold as terror at the heart
That we might fail it.

CHARLES.   Joan, we will not. No.
I have not spoken : I let our Council speak.
Yet the word lies with me. Joan, I will go.
God's voice is with you. Did we not that once
Hear it together? (*To the* COUNCIL) Grudge it not,
    my lords.
You, in your faithful office, doubted; yet
Let her o'ersway your prudence, as she sways
Mine own. We go to take our crown at Rheims.

JOAN (*raising her hands to Heaven*). Joy, joy, that
    all is well, that you have heard !
                      (*Kneels at* DAUPHIN's *feet.*)
Sire, He will never fail His word, for you
Will fail it never. (CHARLES *lays a hand on her hair.*)

TREMOUILLE (*aside*). If she master *him*,
Lost are you, Tremouille. She must win no more
Battles; the charm must sunder. (*Aloud*) Royal lord,
Forgive your Council's doubts. What could we do?
It is a king's right, not a counsellor's,

To venture.   And indeed your confidence
Is venture's soundest warrant.   It will speed.

JOAN (*rising*).   I would you had sped it sooner,
and in name
Of Heaven.

TREMOUILLE.   We statesmen, Maiden, as you said,
Have to walk earth, with pain even that.   The sky
We leave for who can tread it.   Well, perhaps
Our falls are not so costly.

JOAN.   Ah !

TREMOUILLE (*turning to* CHARLES).   My liege,
Will you let draft the summons ?

JOAN (*aside*).   Ay, 'tis hate.
(*To* RAIMOND) O Raimond, mark !
            (*To* DAUPHIN) Your royal Grace has need
Of us no more.

CHARLES.   Till you take horse with me
For Rheims ; but that is soon.   Fair rest the while.

            (JOAN *and* RAIMOND *bow and go.* TRE-
            MOUILLE *talks with* CHARLES.)

JOAN (*going*).   If there befall a treachery, help me
you,
Raimond.

RAIMOND.   O Joan, what's this, then ?

JOAN.   Hush !   Apart.   (*They go.*)

CHARLES (*to* TREMOUILLE).   Content !   Ah, yes ;
so soon could hardly be.

SCENE IV.—Rheims Cathedral, part of the Nave. Citizens, Soldiers, etc.

Enter a Woman *with a child*

WOMAN. God's mercy, here we are. And I thought every bone of little Geoffrey would have been cracked more than ever the Maid could mend him.

SECOND WOMAN. Art crazed to bring that bairn out to-day among the horses!

FIRST WOMAN. Nay, for he'd gotten weak ankle-joints since one-eyed Margot overlooked him. And I said, 'She shall touch him for't.' So I got through with him on my shoulder, and the breath driven out of me by the back end of a pike, and she looked down off the great horse, like an angel out of glory, and patted the head of him.

CITIZEN. The head of him! How's that to cure his feet?

FIRST WOMAN. It be all one either end of him for such as her, and his head was the handier. Look if he do not walk a bit less crooked already.

SECOND WOMAN. Well, I've a lead crown-piece with her graven on it, all in armour, and the standard and the lilies: had it of Friar Luke for a basket of fresh eggs. It's certain 'gainst the shaking fever; and he'll charm it fresh for me every Easter when I take the offerings.

CITIZEN. Leave your chatter, women! Here's the Holy Phial coming. Down on your knees!

(*The Canons of St. Remy, escorted by four gentlemen, carry past the Ampoule.*)

SCOT (*to* JACQUES). What is yonder under the canopy?

JACQUES. Why, what else but the Holy Phial?

SCOT. What's the Holy Phial?

JACQUES. Why, what was brought down to St. Remy's Church out of heaven by a white dove.

FIRST WOMAN. Nay, soldier, 'twas an angel, with gold and blue wings.

JACQUES. Trust a woman to know about angels, and how they be dressed.

SCOT. But what is it for?

JACQUES. Keeps the miracle-oil that makes a dauphin into a king.

SCOT. It will have ado to make a king out of yon, then. I'd blither see the Maid anoint with it.

JACQUES. Whist, man; treason-talk. But, truth, if lying Queen Isabeau, that denied Charles, could have told us Joan was her babe and a boy, there'd be one white deed in a black account. Ay, the stuff for a king! Can teach old Bombard-muzzle himself how to set a battalion, and that without taking ever a curse to it : and gets more work out of mangonels and arblasts than Jean of the Culverin. A girl off a hedge, too !   How comes it, say you ?

BRETON.   Let *me* say.   It is all one tale with her prophesyings.   She was graced straight out of heaven with the fighting, like Peter with the preaching : and 'tis helpfuller for us than preaching.   'Tis the way of the Holy Ghost with her, say I, amen.

(*Crosses himself.*)

JACQUES.   You Bretons be ever pious.   Not that it hinders fighting with you.

Enter MARGUERITE *with* GUY *and* PASQUEREL

MARGUERITE.   Sir, do not fail your station with
        the Peers
For me.   Let Father Pasquerel bring me on.
    GUY.   No, there is time yet.   I must place you
        where
You see the royal sword make knights of us. ,
Then am I doubly cavalier, by stroke
Of the King's sword and of fair Marguerite's eyes.
    MARGUERITE.   Nay, trebly ; Joan will watch it.
        Happy knights !
Guy, did you mark her as she passed the gate
Last even, and the live street broke in voice ?

I think the martyrs born again in bliss
So smile on their awaking.

GUY.   At the feast
Methought she saddened.

MARGUERITE.   Know you why? She heard,
Across the joy-bells, as she rode the street,
A voice on air, 'They will betray thee, Joan;
But fear not'; as she listened on for more,
There was La Tremouille at her stirrup, afoot,
Waiting to help her down.   What make you of it?

GUY.   A fancy.   Fear, on these great heights of joy,
Is human toll for more than human bliss.
Who should betray her?

MARGUERITE.   Wilt be angry with me?

GUY.   No.   You'll not name Laval.

MARGUERITE.   Then tell me, why
Was Tremouille at her stirrup?

GUY.   To help her down.
You said it.

MARGUERITE.   Nay, I cannot like the man.

GUY.   Tut!   He's the oily courtier; 'tis the mode.
No worse.

MARGUERITE.   Guy, listen.   I love the Maid
        almost
As dear as I love any, maid or man.
I would not know the knight who grudged to help
Joan in her peril.

I

GUY. How you look at me!
Should I be like to grudge a perilled dame?
You are not kind.

MARGUERITE. You are so cold for her,
Our Joan, the bravest and most tender soul
God fashioned ever. I could not love the heart
That shut its door upon my other love.

GUY. Do *I* shut door? I see it; you will ask
Raimond, for he's about her most, to play
Your—how to call it?—champion-once-removed.
Doubtless I rank with him but poorly.

MARGUERITE. Guy!
How spleenful! If I answer that I love
Best who best loves the Maid. . . . O, are you dumb?
I can show spleen, I too. Sir, we detain you:
The Father will conduct me. See, they come.
My Lord La Tremouille seeks you: fail him not.

> (GUY *bows stiffly, and they part. Proces-*
> *sion of nobles with* CHARLES *and* JOAN
> *pass through the choir.*)

FIRST WOMAN. Hey! Josephine, never a glimpse
shall we get of it. Sir (*to the* SCOT), ye're kind-hearted
by the face, and you foreign archers be out of common
tall. Heave me up the bairn to your shoulder, to tell
my grandchildren how the Maid looked at the
Crowning.

SCOT. Welcome, good mother. (*Lifts the child.*)

It's not your grandchildren nor his great-great-grand-
children that will set eyes on her match.

SECOND WOMAN. See, gossip, where minstrel
Gautier has climbed to. He's perched on nothing,
like a bird of the air. He will see it all rarely,
unless he happen break his neck sooner.

FIRST WOMAN. Not he; is light of bone as a field-
mouse up a corn-stalk. And there's a providence
for the crazed ones.

> (*A loud music within. As it ends, the voice*
> *of the minstrel is heard.*)
> O by sign of snows and fire,
> O by whispers that aspire. . . .

FRIAR ROBERT. Hush! brother. Hold thy songs,
     and keep thy breath
To tell us here what passes. Are they come
Yet to the altar?

MINSTREL. Yea, the Archbishop mounts
The steps already. There's the Dauphin risen
From prayer, and gone towards him.

FRIAR. He will take
The oath to Holy Church. Heaven guard the same!

MINSTREL. 'Tis sworn. The Peers have said
     amen to it.

CITIZEN. Tell which they be.

MINSTREL. It is quick telling; two—
Clermont, Vendôme.

CITIZEN.   Shame on the stay-aways!

JACQUES.   Patience a moment; there'll be more
anon.

I hear he'll make a Count of young Laval.

SECOND WOMAN.   Ah! that's the merry lad that
came this way,

He and his sweetheart.

FIRST WOMAN.   Eh! 'twas none so sweet
She looked, nor he so merry when he went.

JACQUES.   And after him he makes La Tremouille.

SCOT.   Him!   Well, God keep us.

JACQUES.   And, they say, De Rais.

BRETON.   De Rais!   Why, heart of Mary!   Did
they send

Into our Brittany for the sponsors of him?

JACQUES.   What say'st?   There's never better
man afield.

BRETON.   Ay, sooth, afield.   But do not ask at
home.

For there are Breton fathers—Well, anon.

FRIAR.   Peace, friends, and listen Gautier.

MINSTREL.   Now he knights
The King.

JACQUES.   What he?

MINSTREL.   Alençon.

JACQUES.   Ay, for lack
Of Burgundy.   More shame on Burgundy!

FIRST WOMAN.   Where stands the Maid?

MINSTREL.   On the first altar-step,
At corner; D'Aulon, Raimond, on her left;
And right, her rosy warrior, little Louis
Holds up the banner, with his eyes upon it,
Fair as a boy St. Martin.

FIRST WOMAN.   Bless the child!

MINSTREL.   Now come they to the anointing.
        Mark ye well,
Friends all. . . . The Archbishop from the altar takes
The Holy Phial. . . . The Dauphin kneels again. . . .
The sacred dew pours on him.

FRIAR.   Pray we, friends,
Pray all for grace upon it!   Balm of God
Drawn from the Holiest Holies down on earth
Fall on him, sprinkle him, hallow him to the end!

                    (*A short burst of trumpets.*)

MINSTREL.   Now is he risen.   He turns to front
        the folk.

JACQUES.   How does he bear him?

MINSTREL.   Royally.

SECOND WOMAN.   But his look?
Tell us.

MINSTREL.   How can I that?   Ah, yet I can.
His face is as the Maid's.   And hers—O wonder!

SECOND WOMAN.   Look how the man's o'ercome.

MINSTREL.   A beam on her

Fallen from the skies robes her alone of all
To one white star of glory. . . . Ah, 'tis gone,
And touched none other.

    FRIAR.   'Tis the Maiden's doom.
A woman, travailing, clothèd of the sun.
Alone, alone.   O sinners that be we!

    MINSTREL.   Friends, ye shall shout anon. Give
        heed to me.
One bears the crown to the Archbishop's hand.
He holds it, praying, to the eyes of God.
He sets it on him. Shout! For Charles is King.

            (*Long blast of trumpets. Shout of ' Noel !*
            Noel !')

    FIRST WOMAN.   The Maid, what does she?
    MINSTREL.   Very still is she;
Her eyes uplift, and—O that ye could see!

    MAN.   What is it?
    MINSTREL.   I know not if a miracle!
But up from foot to brows a moving flame
Reddens her armour, sets the Maid on fire.

    FRIAR.   A sign, a sign. What might it token?
    SCOT (*aside*).   Ay,
It is the flame-hued window looking south.
And yet—who knows?

    MINSTREL.   Well, it is passed again,
Like a trance fallen off her; and she wakes.
She falls at the King's knees, embracing them;

I cannot hear her words, but how she sobs,
And how her tears are falling !

JACQUES.   What does he ?

MINSTREL.   Weeps like a child above her.   All
    the Court

Are weeping with her.

FRIAR.   Ah ! the gracious shower.

It is her pity for the realm of France
Makes French hearts tender.   Soft with drops of rain
Is God's inheritance, and the fruit is blessed.

> (*A blast of trumpets.   The procession comes
> back   down   the   nave,   with   shouts   of
> 'Noel !   Noel !'   The* KING *leads* JOAN
> *by the hand.   They pause.*)

CHARLES.   Ah ! Joan, some guerdon of your pains
    is here,

To see our people's gladness.

JOAN.   Dear my liege,

This is a loving people, and a good.
Ah me, how glad in this kind earth of theirs
Would I be laid in dying !

REGNAULT.   Dying, Joan ?

What ails you ?   Know you when your death shall be ?

JOAN.   Ah, no, not I, nor hour, nor place, nor how.

CHARLES.   Then, Joan, what made you say it ?

JOAN.   Can I tell ?

Yet, now the purpose of the Lord is wrought,

Fain were I to go home, so pleased it God
Who made me.   Blithely would I serve again
Father and mother, drive our sheep afield,
Be as my sisters and my brothers are.
And they—how blithely would they have me home !
But O my prince, let come to me what may,
For all is well.   I have done the deed of Christ.

SCENE V. — Ante - chapel of the Church at
    St. Denis, near Paris : the Shrine of
    St. Denis is seen beyond the Screen

TREMOUILLE (*pacing the ante-chapel*).   I trust they
        have taken order at the camp
Ere now.   De Gaucourt was so cowed by her,
I fear him. . . . Yet he plucked her from the
        trench,
And willy-nilly tossed on horse.   Aha !
Then first a Frenchman saw the Maid go back.
We owe him for it.   But I sit on thorns
Till the King's order passes for the march
Homeward.
    MESSENGER.   My lord, De Gaucourt sends you
        word
The camp breaks up at noon.
    TREMOUILLE.   Bear him my thanks.

Inform Sir Raimond that I wait him here
Without the chapel.   (*Exit* MESSENGER.)
                    Then I breathe again.
There's a fight won at last, La Tremouille,
By losing one for her.   The Maid that never,
Never was beaten—beaten at Paris gate !
It is but once : yet in the once is all.
Spells cannot be resoldered. . . . Are we sure ?
I'll keep in quiver still my second shaft,
And use.   It is less cruel : indeed, it is
A shaft of kind Dan Cupid.   O but blunt,
Slack-feathered, one to shame the god !   A wooer,
Raimond, to make men laugh ; but angers more
Me, with his cursèd knightly daintiness
And chivalries of reserve.   I'll make him spring.
If the spring fail, there's matter in the attempt
My wits shall set fermenting.   She has come.
                    (*Looking out of a window.*)
I vanish.

> (*Exit by north door.* JOAN *and* LOUIS,
> *carrying* JOAN'S *armour, enter by south
> door.*)

    JOAN.   Louis, set it down. . . . How chill
The air is of this place.

    LOUIS.   I feel it not,
Dear madam.

    JOAN.   Chill I feel it as the grave.

LOUIS. Your wound has left you weak.

JOAN.   It is not that.

It is the passage of some evil thing
That the touched air gives note of, even as,
Where come the saints, it glows. But gone it is.

                              (*Looks into the church.*)

Yonder the shrine is of St. Denis, right
Of the great altar : you must lay the arms
At Blessed Mary's feet.

LOUIS.   I am very loth.

Will you not tell me why you offer them ?

JOAN. But that you know right well,—in thank-
        fulness
For healing of my wound.

LOUIS.   You said it ; yet

You have been healed before, and did not so.

JOAN. Louis, I heard it said of ancient men
That, when a champion died, they laid his bones,
All in his armour as he fought, beside
The border, 'twixt his people and his foes :
For these could never pass across the sword
Of the dead man, and conquer.

LOUIS.   Speak not so ;

I cannot bear it. You, Maid, are not dead.
You shall not die before your deeds are done.

JOAN. And are you sure that champion was so
        dead

He could do no deed after?   The great Charles,
Yes, Louis, and your holy namesake, fight
Still for their France, being dead.   But let it be.
This armour, shining in the glimmering arch,
Shall tell that hither came our France, and hither
Will come and further, as the river-spoil
Of brimming Seine, left on his meadow, tells
How the shrunk flood can mount there, if he will.

  LOUIS.   Why now, that likes me better.   I will
    bear them
Into the chapel.

  JOAN.   Do; then leave me here.

     (LOUIS *goes into the chapel and places the*
     armour.)

Ah me! what tells my heart that here will be
The loving boy's last service?

  LOUIS (*coming back*).   Maid——

  JOAN.   What is it?

  LOUIS.   I heard De Gaucourt say to Tremouille,
—He meant not to be heard—he said——

  JOAN.   Speak on.

  LOUIS.   Said, 'She is easier handling in the camp
Now,' and he stopped.

  JOAN.   What answered Tremouille?

  LOUIS.   Nothing.   He feigned not hear; he saw
    me.

  JOAN.   So.

My faithful Louis, would you were but half
As strong to help as loyal!

LOUIS.   There be few,
Yet there be some, that love you not.

JOAN.   I know it.
Be silent, Louis, and watch.   But leave me now.

> (LOUIS *goes.*   JOAN *stands at the opening*
> *of the screen.*)

If this should be the end!   If Joan indeed
Must render back again to Him who gave
Arms of his battle; never feel again
The grip of harness make the living nerves
Hard as the steel that girds them.   Should I grieve?
I am so weary of the wars.   At night
When the wound heated me, my dream was still
Of wandering cattle-bells, that seemed to call
Joan to the milking-byre, but when I sought
To follow, there was weight upon my limbs,
Methought of armour, till I looked, and lo!
A chain that girthed me round.   It was the clasp
Of the close bands about the wound, I knew.
But O to smell the fields of home again!

> (*Goes to the door and looks out.*)

Of home.   Ah, yes, after these mighty days.
O I would be yon carolling lark in heaven,
That sings his triumph out on air, and then,
Soft as a dropping plummet, buoys him down

Safe to the nested heather, seen no more.
                    (*Comes back and closes door.*)
Alas! can France be freed except I fight?
Yet, if I fight can she be freed even so,
Except—O Christ! they willed I should not win
At Paris gate : they mock the faith, they mock
In secret.   They will say, 'The Maid has failed.
It was by chance and not by God she won
Those other times.   The charmed sword in her hand,
See, it has broken.'   O, or dare they say,
'Lo, now, she conquered by the Evil One,
Even as we feared'?   Nay, nay, they dare not—yet,
Dear God, what cruel whisper dries my soul,
'Joan, art thou sure?   And cannot Satan clothe
His visiting angels as with light, and work
Signs to deceive the elect, until he draw
A proud heart on to ruin?'   Away, away,
Tempter, I know thee!   Michael, help me thou,
And holy Catherine, holy Margaret, help!
Sweet sisters mine of Paradise, on earth
Comfort the mortal maiden : speak with her.
                (*She kneels.   A bell begins to toll.   She
                looks up suddenly.*)
Spake ye?   Yea, yea : the light, the light!   O nigher,
Come nigher : I fear not, I.   Great Son of light,
Strong Seraph of the Sword of Heaven, O speak,
Speak, for the Maiden hears. . . .

Yea, Lord, I know it.   Alas! it was not done.
But could I do your bidding, if the men
Denied me yonder?   How I strove, thou knowest:
And sure I am ye have all forgiven me.
What then;   what next?   Ah, clearer!   Let me
   hear
And understand. . . . Thy sword!   Yea, thine was
   never
Broken.   O, I will follow, follow again.
But how is this?   What meanest?
Not with the blade thou beckonest as before.
Why hold'st to me the hilt, a shining cross
Of flame, aglow yet from thine hand? or is it
Jewelwork, as they fashion gems in heaven,
Of living fire?   Have pity: I cannot look.

         (*Veils her eyes.*)

'Believe—endure'?   Yea, to the end, the end,
That will I, thou beside me.
Kind Sisters of the Glory, succour me:
I kept the faith unbroken, and the vow.
. . . Ah, leave me not alone, stay with me yet,

       (*Reaches out her arms.*)

Or bear me in your tender arms away
Where no more war is. . . . Gone!   O sorrow, sorrow!
I would have wept my heart out at their feet,
Clutching those skirts of brightness—and 'tis gone.

         (*Rises.*)

I'll go (for they will hear me still) and pray
Beside my harness in St. Denis' shrine.

> (*Goes to the shrine and kneels.*)

TREMOUILLE *and* RAIMOND *enter the ante-chapel*

TREMOUILLE.   We should make leisure, since our
    talk is done,
To find the priest and view his treasures. . . . Ah !

> (*Calls* RAIMOND'S *attention to* JOAN *in
> distance.*)

We should intrude to enter.   Yet perhaps
The sight we chance on more concerns than all
St. Denis' heirlooms.   Or how read you this?
    RAIMOND.   My lord, I think the Maid would be
    alone.
    TREMOUILLE.   We will forbear.   And yet one
    word ; you note
How, dedicating here yon arms, she counts
Her soldier-mission done.
    RAIMOND.   It may be so.
    TREMOUILLE.   'Tis common knowledge ; but she
    seals it now.
And what were left to do,—for her, I mean?
    RAIMOND.   Paris is left.
    TREMOUILLE.   We clutched the fruit unripe.
'Twill fall, let pass a season.   And the Maid

Has taught us win.   All else will come, and she
Will rest the while,—and keep a good knight's house.
May he be worthy!   Well, I go; but you,
Doubtless, attend her.   (*Is going, but returns.*)
                              Sir, occasion stays
For no man.   Take an elder's word, and dare.
                                        (*Exit.*)
      RAIMOND.   How meant he that?   For may I
        trust him?   Good
He is not, yet discerning.   Loves her not
(How could he love a spirit sphered beyond
That measured field of statecraft where his own
Walks and is sure?), yet her he hates not, me
Would prosper, as he deems prosperity.
Sound earnest of his mind I have.   And then
She has achieved; he spoke but truth; her hour
Of mission ends; she is sweet Joan again,
A tender woman, and disarmoured, see,
Of that divine encompassment that held
Violence aloof and vileness.   Ah, the fear!
She knows it; she will need me.   Dare I will!
                (*JOAN rises and comes down the church.*)
O heart, be strong to let me speak!   She comes.
A storm has swept those eyes, and leaves of it
But the clear shining after.   (*JOAN reaches him.*)
                              Maid, I wait
To be your comrade home.

JOAN.   Most timely met!
Fain am I of a comrade.

    RAIMOND.   Say ye that?
O 'tis an omen.   Ere yon door is passed,
Joan, there's a word to speak, that must be spoke
Now—here.   I have kept it silent week on week;
It had been sin to utter.   But the hour
O'ertakes us.   You have laid your arms away:
God sets you free to rest; but rest you cannot
Safe (nay, you know it) in our violent land,
Except—.   O Joan, your servant am I, see
If I can knightlier serve, than with my life
Bar out your peril,—so you vouch the name
That makes my life your own.

    JOAN (*takes his two hands and holds them*).   Why,
        Raimond, this has happened in a dream
Long since.   For dream it was; a girl that sat
Beside a river, and a gallant boy
That would have offered love, but out of heaven
The scaring flame fell.   It is safer here,
Under these arches, than the oaken bough;
Yet perilous, if the kind saints look not on.
But now—sworn Maiden am I, sworn to them,
So long as God desire it.   Yet I love,
—Yea, truly, after Christ and the pure saints,—
All men, and Raimond of our Domremy
The most.   But how one woman loves one man

              K

No guess have I, long as God wills me Maid,
So help me Maid St. Catherine.   And for this—
It is a dream, a dream come back again,
My friend, three summers after.

   RAIMOND.   Ay, a dream
That blasts your friend in breaking.

   JOAN.   Raimond, why?

   RAIMOND.   Because the friend that dared be more
    than friend,
Being forbid, must go, not help you more.

   JOAN.   I will not suffer it; you shall not go.

   RAIMOND.   How else?   You cannot keep me
    with you still.

   JOAN.   Why not?   It was a dream that happened
    here.
The dreamers will not tell, and none can know.
And the wise clerks, that write our time in books,
Will never write how the true Raimond loved
Idly, but nobly, and for France and God
Made love forbid die into faith, and wrought,
Beside his sister of the Holy Will,
All God's fair pleasure out.   Is love so great,
So great a thing this love of man for maid,
That, breaking, it should break the man?   Ah! no.
And, Raimond, there is left so much for us
To work together.   They were here but now,
They said, 'Believe—endure.'   They said not, 'Rest.'

There. You have waked. It was a dream. Come on
Abroad, and look on a new morrow's face.
> *(Leads to the door.)*
RAIMOND. I am yet more in dreams. Yet I will
 come.

SCENE VI.—A HALL IN THE CASTLE OF SULLY

TREMOUILLE reading a state-paper

TREMOUILLE. I moved a thought too plainly.
 Foiled once more
Is our Invincible; but, if men see
The hand that foiled her—? How mine own tame
 bull
De Gaucourt snorts! I wonder if his nose
Have found the ring in it I lead him by.
He scared our holy Regnault yesterday
With most indecent cursing for the stint
Of men and means to storm La Charitè.
I moved too plain; it must be covered.
 MARGUERITE *(entering)*.   Sir!
 TREMOUILLE. All at your service, damsel.
 MARGUERITE.   If it break
No secret, when shall I expect the Maid?

TREMOUILLE.　I am left to guess.　You also?
　　　This is slack
Remembrance of her friends.
MARGUERITE.　　　　　　　　I think she had
No heart for messages.
TREMOUILLE.　　　　You magnify,
Surely, her failure.
MARGUERITE.　　Hers!　We thought the blame
(What knows a woman?) was the succourers.
They marched so late, 'tis murmured.
TREMOUILLE.　　　　　　　　Talk they so?
When was France beaten ever but the folk
Railed at their chiefs?　Our men are conquerable
Like others.
MARGUERITE.　Not our maids, or so believe
The captains (what can women know?); they say
The King should clear her name of the mischance.
TREMOUILLE.　Fair dame, we'll have you of the
　　　council, you
So overtake our wisdom.　Here's a scroll,
—No, for I must not show it—but it speaks
Your very mind out.
MARGUERITE.　　Then 'tis well: yet pity
That e'er we need it.　Had La Charitè
But been Saint Pierre again!　And wherefore not?
Was Joan less forced with angels?
TREMOUILLE.　　　　　　　Why, for me

The muster roll of tramping men-at-arms
Is task enough; these levies of the air
Baffle my reckoning.

MARGUERITE. Ah! you did not laugh
When Gerard told the story. But I stay
Your business.

TREMOUILLE. Damsel, no; but as you will.

(*She goes.*)

'The captains.' Ay, they speak their mind with her.
Am *I* so sure our Maid is conquerable?
My love-trap has not snared her; curse on him,
The maiden-mettled boy I lured her with.
And this defeat in field recoils on me.
See here: (*Reads from the paper.*) 'The King pro-
    nounces graciously'
(And I must prompt him to it, and write the same)
'For late achievements of the Noble Maid,
Albeit of fortune crossed, without reproach
Of valour or of leadership, his thanks
Most full and loving?' Then she wins again.
There. (*Tears the paper.*) Could I tear the record
    of her so!
Could I but shred this bond of Maid and King
And burn it, as these tatters!

(*Throws the paper into the fire.*)

Fool! 'Tis not like yourself, La Tremouille,
To ease your heart in fury: curse on her

That puts you to't. 'The captains'! Do they love
So well ? O yes, and there be captains too
Persuadable to hatred. Envy might
Do more than foemen to relieve us. . . . Ha ! . . .
Save she be charmed. . . . How could those English
    else
Miss her, alone, under their bows, the rest
Run from her side ? . . . 'Her angels.' O, for-
    sooth,
That fable thrives ; a 'fifty thousand,' was it ?
And not a sorry devil helping me !
Too good belike, to earn it, I. My heart
In truth does something ail at moments when
I mark—. The spite of Heaven to tempt a man
So ! . . . But the girl must under and not I.

Gr-r-r- ! to go pen those loving thanks anew.

                        (*Goes.*)

SCENE VII.—A Room in Compiègne

Marguerite *alone, working an embroidery*

Marguerite (*holding up the work to look at it*).
    Well, there's my Joan, done to the very spurs.
The sorry picture ! Who could work those eyes
With thread and needle ? But herself will come

To-morrow.   Lord! and what a wheel is life!
Here comes it round.   Marguerite besieged again ;
Only the town is Compiègne ; and Joan
Rides in again to chase them.   And the time
May-month again.   All good begins with spring.

Enter LOUIS

Louis!   Joan's Louis here in Compiègne!
Or is this Orleans, and the year a dream
I wake from where it started?   No, for you
Had redder cheeks last May-time.
  LOUIS.   Is it so?
Well, Marguerite, I was sick a fortnight since,
And rose but lately.   How you stared!   But I
Knew you should come from Sully with the Dame
Of Trèves.   O could you know how glad am I!
  MARGUERITE.   Sick were you?   That's amiss.   But,
   for the rest,
How like you the Archbishop?
  LOUIS.   Like him!   Talk
Of something else.
  MARGUERITE. Not I.   Why like you not?
  LOUIS.   He is so vain.
  MARGUERITE.   Why, so may good men be.
  LOUIS.   Well, then, he makes me carry in the book
Beside him at the vespers.

MARGUERITE.   When of course
You would be quoiting.

LOUIS (*rising and coming close*).   Marguerite, the
    man—
I'll tell it you ; we are such friends—I say,
He is a devil in lawn and velvet : there !

MARGUERITE (*rising too, and taking his hand*).
    What is it, Louis, what is it ?

LOUIS.   Judge yourself.
I waited as he supped ; the captain sat
Beside him (know you what this Flavy is ?) :
The people clamoured in the street : a voice
Rang thro' the casement, ' Send for Joan ; the folk
Will have their Joan to lead them.'   O to see
Grow purple on Flavy's cheek the scar he got
In killing of young Thibault in the wood,
When—

MARGUERITE.   What is that of Thibault ?

LOUIS.   Ay, who knows ?
Men whisper Thibault's sister was too fair
And good, howe'er that made it.   But he flushed
With envy !   Beast !   What cares he for the town
Except as Flavy's harvest-field that grows
A marshal-staff for Flavy.

MARGUERITE.   Well, and then ?

LOUIS.   He cursed her thro' the bristles on his lip,
Softly.   The Archbishop (*him* I hate the worst)

Waved his embroideries, eyed his ruby, said,
' Humour your honest people ; let her come.
Always you are captain of our forces here :
They'll do or not do by your order, and she—
She is so headlong in the field.'   And there,
Altho' I stood behind him, yet I knew,
His lashes lifted, and the captain's fell,
As if he thought on something.   When he thinks,
Marguerite, 'tis always of a villainy.

    MARGUERITE.   You cast me in a terror.   Four
        days back
I know there came a post from Tremouille,
And very secret.   Half an hour therefrom
Regnault was close with Flavy, came away
Smiling, as when he seals the last despatch
That fools Good Philip, and reconquers France.
O Joan, if Regnault be as vile as vain !
But what to do ?

    LOUIS.   Let Guy that comes with her—
For you will wed him—no ?

    MARGUERITE.   Peace, Louis, on that.
(*Aside*) She'll not believe him—Tremouille's kin.
        Ah yes,
Raimond, would Guy but help him ;—alack, but he
Is jealous—all my doing—fears I'll wed
Whichever of the two will help the Maid.
Certainly so I told him : silly one,

To take my word, when half a lover's eye
Might show him Raimond is a sillier yet,
And still goes hoping—Lord! the folly!—(*turns to*
    Louis.) Yes,
Guy must be told, and Louis, do it you.

    Louis. Soon said. But, if she come, my lord
    will find
He cannot spare me from his side, the false,
Sleek, scented, satin-fingered, purring cat!
O how I wish that I were wicked enough
To spice its fish some Friday!

    Marguerite.   O sir knight!

    Louis (*laughs*). Yes, there's the pity. For what
    other way
Has poor page Louis? Well, no more of him.
We'll talk of Joan, from whom he carried me.
                      (*Sits at her feet.*)
That hateful Sully, could she brook it?

    Marguerite.   No;
So sore she fretted, that they set the cage
Open awhile. St. Pierre she took by storm,
And would have stormed La Charitè, but then,
As one might loose a falcon in a string
And pluck it from the stroke, so they with her.

    Louis. Who dared do that?

    Marguerite.   Why, Louis, to take up
Your dainty phrase about your friend in lawn,

It was your devil-master's master-devil.
Now need I name him?

    LOUIS.   No.

    MARGUERITE.   Nor name him you,
Sweet Louis, for your life's sake.

    LOUIS.   Well, and next?

    MARGUERITE.   One morn in March she vanished
        with her squires.
The King might whistle and the Councillor;
Their bird would never come to wrist and wear
Their bells and jesses more.   She sails the sky,
To soar and view and stoop and strike at will.

    LOUIS.   O glorious!   That was Joan.   Ah me!
        to hold
A banner o'er the lion-hearted Maid,
And then a canopy for this prowling fox!
Marguerite, for pity, stop my mouth, before
I break my dear lost lady's ordinance
With cursing—

    MARGUERITE.   And in time too.   (*Touches him.*)

Enter FLAVY

                    Sir, you seek
The Archbishop?   He shall hear.
                    (*She and* LOUIS *are going.*)

    FLAVY.   No, pray you, not

Leave your embroidering yet.   His gentleman
Will pleasure us. (LOUIS *goes.*) Our Compiègne gives,
            I fear,
Blank welcome to the dames whose visit finds
Our hands so full with Philip's.

    MARGUERITE.   There is one
Whose visit will be welcome more for Philip's.

      FLAVY. Ah, the Maid-Marshal.   Do we count
            her dame?
She is rather for our wars than pleasures.

    MARGUERITE.   Yes.

      FLAVY.   You speak as having marked it.

    MARGUERITE.   I, sir? No.
Only I heard that, when she tarried last,
Some revels of your Compiègne gallantry
Seemed—shall I say, too gallant?—and she said it.
But, pardon; let me seek the Chancellor,
Since Louis fails. (*Aside*) Folly, to prick him thus
Against her!   Yet to see him and forbear—
Who could?   (*Exit, passing* REGNAULT, *who enters.*)

      FLAVY. My lord, she comes to-morrow, as you
            heard.
I take your counsel for the event of clash
Of Maid's and Captain's orders.

    REGNAULT.   You must walk
Warily, sir. The heads of captains sit
Loose on their shoulders now, since Franquet's fell

Upon the Lagny dunghill.   And for what?
Murder and plunder?   These are names of war.
Few leaders of our own dare cast the crime
At Franquet.   Rape?   Sir, you will grant with me
Our own battalions are not monasteries.
It vastly pleased the Lagny rabble.   Yes;
Your folk adore her too.   The precedent,
Which slays an officer at a rabble's nod,
Should make our leaders thoughtful; they must do
So much a rabble cannot wisely judge.
I wonder now if it was all in jest
She warned Dunois, 'obey or lose his head.'
I am sorry, sir, for your embarrassments.

    FLAVY.   I thank you much.   They will sit
        lighter if
You tender one assurance.   Here to North
The Second Council is the King; to you
Is my account to make.   If any chance
(As with this frantic girl may happen well)
Cause her miscarriage, and the gutter yelps
For Flavy's blood, have I to fear or no?

    REGNAULT.   O, she will not miscarry.   Fear not
        that.

    FLAVY.   I do not *fear* it,—but it may befall.
                       (*A silence.*)
Will my account in it stand safe with you?
                       (*A silence.*)

REGNAULT.   De Gaucourt shut a door on her ; the
      mob
Came nigh to stoning him.

FLAVY.   If *I* shut doors
In duty's name, I'll front the mob, no fear,
So that they get not at my back.   I ask,
Are you behind me, in that pinch, my lord ?

                                  (*A silence.*)

REGNAULT.   Why, that is just.

FLAVY.   Your hand on it, my lord.

SCENE VIII.—COMPIÈGNE.   A PLATFORM ON THE
    RAMPARTS, LOOKING OVER RIVER.   A BRIDGE
    IS SEEN BELOW, WITH A FORTALICE ON THE
    FARTHER SIDE, AND BEYOND IT A CAUSEWAY
    RUNS TOWARDS THE POSITIONS OF THE BUR-
    GUNDIANS.

JOAN *scanning the country, and* SOLDIERS

D'AULON (*entering*).   Your   troop   is   mustered,
    Maid, and at command.

JOAN.   Are ye well rested all ?

D'AULON.   As if the night
Had passed in bed, not saddle.

JOAN.   Well is that.

This evening's gallop is not far, but fierce.
Look, D'Aulon.   From this bridge the causeway runs
A straight mile thro' the floods, to where the Duke
Centres his host in Margny.   More to right
Clairvoix is his, and to the left Venette
Lodges those English.   All the camp's at ease,
Thinks the day done ; for see those strollers there,
And circles at the fires.   When opes our gate,
We'll pounce ; and e'er they gather up their wits
Yon lilies flutter over Margny cross.

                (*Low applause of* SOLDIERS.)

D'AULON.   And after ?

JOAN.   There are scarce three hours to dusk.
We trench us strong in Margny, 'twixt their wings
Venette and Clairvoix.   Hands they cannot join
Across our sword between.   Let either stir,
As I do think for very fear they must,
To grope for his ally thro' darkness, we
Spring once again, and end them.   Is it well?

    D'AULON.   As always.   And we'll do it.   Flavy
        spares
Two hundred of his own.

    JOAN.   'Tis strong indeed.
Ourselves and our good friends of Compiègne
Stirrup by stirrup, who could stop the way?

    D'AULON.   He has lined the current left and right
        the bridge

With archer-folk on barges, as you asked,
Against a need.

    JOAN.   Good. (*Whispers*) Is he honest then?

    D'AULON. Who knows? None ever knew the
        thoughts behind

That front of founded iron.

    JOAN.   Well, to work.

Enter RAIMOND *with his arm bound up*

No, Raimond, no. How should your sword-hand
    draw,
Fresh from that lance-thrust?

    RAIMOND.   Yes, but let me see it.

    JOAN. Why, so you shall, as all will, from the wall.
No, friend; at dawn you scarce could sit your horse.
I post you here. . . . . My banner there!

                      (*They show it.*)
                      The day
Comes round,—for is it not Ascension-eve?—
When first it looked on fight. (*Aside*) But where is
    gone
The fair face under it once? They steal my friends,
And hide them from me.   (*Looks towards town.*)
                Nay but that is strange!
                  (*Waves her hand.*)

    RAIMOND. Whom see you yonder?

JOAN.   See not you ?   My stout
And tender knight of the White Banner, Louis.
He beckons from a window, where, I think,'
They prison him from speech with me.   (*Aside*)
     Farewell.
At feast to-morrow you shall sit by Joan.
(*Aloud*) We tarry.   Hear Rolande, who stamps for
     me
I' the gateway.   Let them slip the bolts.   My friends,
                                   (*To the people.*)
Pray for us while you watch ; but ere I come,
Have out your gauds and braveries every one,
And drape your streets too.   Let the ringers be
Your deftest, for I'll bring a noble guest.
                            (*To the* SOLDIERS.)
My men, be merry of your hunt to-day ;
We'll bring Duke Philip in to Compiègne !
               (JOAN *and* SOLDIERS *descend from the
               ramparts.*)
     ONE OF THE CROWD.   Make   for   the   eastward
          buttress ; there one sees
Down into Margny Market.
     ANOTHER.   Have with you !
     RAIMOND (*left alone*).   Duke Philip !   Sooth, she
          knows the fighting-man.
How the blithe vaunt will send the blood a-boil
Up the grim fellow's sword-arm to his hilt.

                         L

Duke Philip! . . . And who knows? . . . And, if it
    falls,
O heaven and earth! then are our wars at end.
It is but Philip weights the English scale.
We'd draw it in a twinkling. Raimond, then,—
Then Joan is free. Yea, 'while God wills me Maid';
So went it. Heart, be still! . . . And Tremouille
    gives
The promise of his word with Charles for me.
A peer of France! And then to lay the prize
Down at her feet, the crown of womanhood.
O heart, be still, I bid you, lest you burst
With throbbing o'er this tourney and the stake.

              (*He leans over the wall.*)

Here come they thro' the port. With what a
    stride
Moves the tall charger on the bridge! I know
His great heart's beating to the banner's flap;
The music of her bounding valour has set
His strong limbs dancing, as if air were filled
With trumpet-blowings, tho' no breath is blown,
So silent creeps the column to the shock.

           (GUY, *approaching, touches him.*)

Ah, Guy, what is it?

GUY.   Would I knew! but ill.
I was in Regnault's house; young Louis caught
My hand in a dark passage, whispered quick,

'She is betrayed; tell Raimond; O keep eyes
On Flavy'; then he vanished, as my lord
Came from a creaking doorway.   What's to do?
    RAIMOND.   'Betrayed,'—and 'Flavy'!   Truth, he
        hates her well,
So frank she was.   But he would never risk
His town's best helper.
    GUY.   Does he think her that?
Flavy will save it surely, but by Flavy:
She stands between the sunlight and his fame.
I cannot leave the charge I took of him
(Judge why he chose it) by yon counter-gate.
Watch you the bridge and port, O Raimond, watch!
                                 (Goes.)
    RAIMOND.   And Tremouille sent message, ere we
        came,
Commending me to Flavy, let him know
The King had given me secret charge—O no;
That child is stuffed with fears from some one's
        hint,
Who scents the Captain's envy, dreams the rest.
Well, I will watch.   Yet ill it were to break
With Tremouille by a fool suspicion, and wreck
Hopes that are Joan's if mine. . . . Their camp is
        roused,
And swarming like an ant-hill stirred, but how
Disorderly; she'll sweep it at a touch.

Enter JACQUES

Yes, Jacques, to watch is torture.

JACQUES.   'Tis not that.
I cannot fathom yonder archer-folk,
That man the barges.   I'd have had them drop
Cable, and cross, and hold a pole's length off
The meadow-bank.   How shall they help us else,
If the pinch comes?   And, mark, sir, if the Maid
Be not at standstill.

RAIMOND.   Jacques, go find me where
The Captain stands.   (JACQUES *goes.*)
                    I'll warn him.   Yet I think
He's not the fighter, he, to leave a joint
Loose in his harness. . . . Brave!   They give again
Before us.   Onward!   onward!   Yes, the Banner
Has cleared the meadow-belt that stayed us.

SCOT (*entering*).   ˙Sir.

RAIMOND.   You bring a message.

SCOT.   No.

RAIMOND.   What would you then?

SCOT.   They sent me from my post, Sir Raimond.

RAIMOND.   Well?

SCOT.   She had set me at yon outwork gate, that
    guards
The bridge.   It keeps their entry backward.

RAIMOND.   Well?

SCOT.   They put the Captain's varlet in my place.

RAIMOND.   What then?

SCOT.   Red Grègory speared Sir Claude, they
    say;

And Flavy would not hang him.

RAIMOND.   Have you more?

SCOT.   I saw the Maid go past me yestereve.

RAIMOND.   You! here in Compiègne!   She was
    not come.

SCOT.   She passed me, sir, from left to right, her
    hands

Bound.

RAIMOND.   O, a dream!   I understood not.

SCOT.   Dream!

Sir, I was sentinel on the bridge.   The clock

Struck six.

RAIMOND.   Ah, bowman,—then?

SCOT.   She passed again

From right to left, but shrouded; and the shroud

A pillar of thick smoke. . . . Alack!   See there.

            (*Both look out towards Margny.*)

They push us out of Margny.

RAIMOND.   Help her Heaven!

O yet she'll rally!

SCOT.   Nay, but bring them back

Safe.   'Tis enough.   She did from Noyon bridge

When our night-onset missed.

RAIMOND.   Ah ! that is she
Last, but for D'Aulon's roan abreast of her,
With Pothon, if I know him by the helm.
That sorrel is her brother's, is it not ?
    SCOT.   Ay.   They be half way home.   And how
    she holds
Her troop, unhurrying as a tourney-show.
    RAIMOND.   Yet the swords bite.   Those troopers
    of the Duke
Flinch, mark it ! from the grapple.   All is well.
          (MINSTREL, *unseen, is heard singing.*)

        MINSTREL.

    Is it man can prick the armour
        Of the Lord ?
    Is it foe can reach to harm her
        With the sword ?
    Nay, 'tis hand of France can lure her,
    Nay, 'tis friend can smite her surer
        With the word.

    FLAVY (*on the ramparts*).   Ho there, within the
    gates !   Stand to the chains !
    SCOT (*aside*).   Is that the 'word'?   (*Aloud*) There's
    mischief, sir, abroad ;
Can smell it on the wind.   What means his sword
              (*Indicating* FLAVY.)

Bared, see you, when no fight's afoot for us?
I'll swear 'tis for some villain signalling.
Quick, sir, they're close! Canst see the star
    upon
Her charger's front.

    RAIMOND (*goes up to* FLAVY). Sir Captain, let me
      take
A score of men to help her at the gate,
If there come trouble.

        (*Cries of crowd, ' We'll go, we'll go.' ' Take
      me, sir.'*)

FLAVY.   Could ye reach her now?
Her troop has choked the bridge-head.

RAIMOND.   Will you, then,
Signal your archers on the stream to shoot?

FLAVY. And riddle the fair lady and your friends?
I pray you, sir, stand wide. You hinder me.

        (*They move apart*).

SCOT (*whispers* RAIMOND). God's name! I see
    it. He'll shut yon outwork door,
And leave the Maid afield. One thing's to do;
Cry 'treason' and rush down upon the gate.
The folk are with us, and one cry of it
Will hold the villain's hands.

    RAIMOND (*aside*).   And if it be
A folly, then I lose her.

    SCOT.   Quick, O quick!

RAIMOND. Maid's men, around me! Treason! there is treason!

Follow me to the gate!

CROWD. We will, we will!

Treason! a treason!

(RAIMOND, *going, is met by* FLAVY.)

FLAVY. How! What hubbub's here?

RAIMOND. There be false men among us; seize them you.

FLAVY. Sir, if I find them. Am I Captain here, Or you? To riot upon my walls! And see,

(*Points sword towards bridge-head.*)

She's but a spear-length off the fortalice door: She comes safe in.

RAIMOND. Ah, if it be but so!

(JOAN'S *voice heard.*)

To me! to me! Rally, O rally!

(*A crash of the city gate closing.*)

RAIMOND. God!

The bridge is risen,—the fort is shut on her,—

They have her! (*Roar of Burgundians heard.*)

Devil! and you bade them do it.

FLAVY. Ho there, arrest him!

CROWD. Friend of the Maid! Ye shall not.

FLAVY. Sir, you are King's man, else—. When gave I word?

They shut it in their fear; the chance of war.

I cannot parley; to your stations all.

             (FLAVY, SOLDIERS, *etc., move off.* RAIMOND
             and SCOT *remain.*)

SCOT.   Sir, I will follow you to the world's end,
      ay,

The very Devil's door, to get her back.

RAIMOND.   Too late !

SCOT.   And drink this Flavy's blood.

RAIMOND.   Too late !

ACT III

SCENE I.—The Hall of the Castle at Rouen,
arranged for a Court

A few assessors already seated

Enter Isambard de la Pierre *and a* Doctor,
meeting.

Doctor.   You, De la Pierre! You did not sit
    with us
Yesterday.

Isambard.   Bitter loth I came to-day.
Think'st they will push it to the death?

Doctor.   How not?
'Tis God or Satan speeds her. If the first,
Then damned is England for outfacing her.
If Satan, burn she must. And, to the herd
No proof of guilt will be one half so plain,
As being plainly burnt for it. Besides,

More price, more prized; and England bought her dear
(Think, 'twas a prince's ransom) from the Duke.
To buy the candle for the game, and then
Not light it, were unthrifty. No, she dies.

ISAMBARD. That she should die by Frenchmen,
she the pride
Of France, if Frenchmen were their own again!

DOCTOR. Treason, dear schoolfellow. But fear
not me:
Fear Cauchon. Ill it is to stand between
A hungry man and his—Archbishopric.

ISAMBARD. Is that his wage?

DOCTOR. Why, yes; his wage, until
Come wage-day. Then,—well, there's the Pope to
please
And dour dogs of the Rouen Chapter—Stay,
Yon patched gown of your Order creeping past,
Who is it?

ISAMBARD. You to ask! Lemaitre, the Vicar
Of the Holy Office, that will share the bench
With Cauchon.

DOCTOR. Bench! the footstool, if you will.
Poor mole, how dazed abroad! But he can blink
His mum assent to Cauchon's ay or no!
And what is wanted more?

ISAMBARD. How went the Court
Those other sessions?

DOCTOR. Do not make me tell.
They bade her ('tis the touchstone for a witch)
Repeat the Pater Noster. She demurred.
It went against her reverence, as I think,
To do't in open court. But then she cried,
'O Father, be my Confessór to-night,
And gladly will I speak it.' Sir, to see
The sick squirm of our Is-to-be-Archbishop
Around the arrow where she lodged it in
What for another man had been the heart.
Faugh! Do not ask me. Let us choose a seat.

(*They move to the chairs.*)

MANCHON (*affecting to inspect the secretaries' table*).
Honest oak boards and not cloth enough to cover
a five-foot eavesdropper! Where are you and I to
hide to-day?

COLLES. Peace, friend! Let a man forget it.
My hand smells of that job still. They'll come
hunting her to-day, not trapping.

TAQUEL. Ah,—say you?

MANCHON. What see'st?

TAQUEL. Look not o'er your shoulder, and I'll
tell you. There's a curtain three parts across the
north window. 'Tis to keep the sun out at mid-day,
belike. And the Dame Seneschal's cat has kittened
in the fold of it; or 'tis a man's elbow bulges it.

MANCHON. Elbow! Then square yours, my

masters, and fill your sheet with street-rhymes or
scrabble. 'Tis all one for the Process.

TAQUEL. And, by Beelzebub, that cursed Loiseleur
has his chair before the gap of it. But, Lord love
you, don't follow my eyes, or he'll scent that I scent
him.

COLLES. Beelzebub douse him deep, when his
time comes! He went nigh to damning you and me,
William, with that trick behind the arras, in the poor
wench's cell.

MANCHON. Damned in good company, then;
you in a bishop's lap and I in an English Millourt's.

COLLES. Will she know her prison-fellow again in
his cassock?

TAQUEL. Scarce that. Yet she might nose him,
if he had not taken a back seat on the far side of
Cauchon; but that blinds the scent for her. Hush!

CAUCHON, *with his principal assessors, enters and
takes his seat*

CAUCHON.   Doctors and Reverend Sirs, I pay my
          thanks
For your full muster here to-day, to God's
More glory. Next I welcome to his chair
My partner in this weighty charge, the Vicar
In Rouen of the Holy Office, whom,

Now that his powers at last are warranted,
I thus present to you.   We shall proceed
As heretofore by interrogatory
Of the accused.   (*An assessor whispers him.*)
                Ah ! you remind me well.
Stand forward, usher Massieu.

    MASSIEU.   Here, my lord.

    CAUCHON.   It is reported you permit the girl
To worship in the Chapel.

    MASSIEU.   She did beg
A moment's stay in passing at the door
To see the Christ on the altar ; nothing more.

    CAUCHON.   Suffer it on your peril, sir, again.
Go now and bring her.   (MASSIEU *goes.*)
                I have heard she cleaves
Still to the scandal of her man's attire.

    ISAMBARD (*to* DOCTOR).   Less man, I fear me,
                were less maid among
Such keepers, friend.

    DOCTOR.   O, he's an innocent,
Our Cauchon.   How should he divine ?   And she—
I think she'd easier burn than break it to him.

                (JOAN *is brought in.*)

    CAUCHON.   Give her again the oath.

    JOAN.   Have I not sworn
Already ?

    CAUCHON.   You shall swear again.

JOAN. Why then,
Again I say it; I may not answer all,
But that which God allows me.

CAUCHON. Swear to answer
Whatso concerns this trial.

JOAN (*touching the Book*). That I swear.

CAUCHON. Now shall you tell us why you come
again
Clothed thus against the wont and modesty
Of woman.

JOAN. God will have it.

CAUCHON. God command
This shame of womankind!

JOAN. He knoweth why
Need is to wear it still.

CAUCHON. Then you are charged
With bearing rings for blameful use.

JOAN. Ah yes!
My lord, you took the ring, my father's gift.
I pray you give't me back, or sell it you
To comfort some poor woman with an alms.

CAUCHON. A tool of sorceries! Heaven forbid!
. . . They say
Your banner, Joan, had spells enwoven on it.

JOAN. Spells? There was Jesu's name, and
Mary's there:
No more.

CAUCHON. We know your soldiers made them
          flags
After its pattern, and by charm of these
They won their fights.

JOAN.   O sirs; there was no charm.
I called, 'Go in among yon English, friends,'
And I went in the foremost.   That was all.

ENGLISH LORD. Saint George! A gallant girl!
          Were she but ours!

ISAMBARD (*aside*).   She's ours; and thus we
          honour her!

CAUCHON.   'Tis averred
They waved your banner at the sacring time
Over your prince's head.

JOAN.   I saw not that.

CAUCHON.   It   stood   beside   God's   altar,   it
          alone,
Of all your nobles' banners. Was it well?

JOAN.   Yea; it had seen the travail, was it not
Meet it should see the glory?

ENGLISH LORD.   Brave again!
'Swounds! but she pays them rarely!

CAUCHON.   Good my lords,
I must entreat you more respect the Court,
In justice' name.

ENGLISH LORD (*aside*).   'Justice'!   He means,
          the Devil's!

MANCHON (*to* TAQUEL).   Our Cauchon strutting
    'neath an English nose !
What makes the cock so pert ?

TAQUEL.   Beshrew your tongue !
Dost know how quick his ears are ?

MANCHON.   Do I not ?
So it be behind an arras.

TAQUEL.   Fool, be still.

CAUCHON.   I charge the learned doctor John
    Beaupere
To question further.

BEAUPERE.   You shall tell me, Joan,
First of this Voice.

JOAN.   So that you ask me not
For things I may not speak.

BEAUPERE.   When came it last ?

JOAN.   This morn, upon my waking.

BEAUPERE.   Spake it near,
And in the room ?

JOAN.   I know not, but it spake
Somewhere within the Castle.

BEAUPERE.   How mean you that ?

JOAN.   Like a great bell it came from everywhere.

BEAUPERE.   And said ?

JOAN.   ' Be bold to answer them.'

BEAUPERE.   No more ?

JOAN.   ' Be bold, for God is with you.'

M

(*Turning to* CAUCHON.)   Sir, my judge,
Have care of your own self.   Indeed I come
From God, and sore in peril shall you be
Who judge me.

CAUCHON (*to* BEAUPERE).   Pass we forward.

BEAUPERE.   Next I ask,
Hast ever seen his form that speaks with you?

JOAN.   You mean the holy Michael?

BEAUPERE.   If't be he.

JOAN.   Of him I told you; these men wrote it
        down.

BEAUPERE.   Yet tell it once again.   What form
        had he?

JOAN.   Manlike, but very noble.

BEAUPERE.   And his voice?

JOAN.   Was noble.

BEAUPERE.   But his speech? has ever spoken
In English tongue?

JOAN.   My faith! how would he that?
He is not of the party of the English.

MANCHON (*to* TAQUEL).   Ah, but a hit for Joan,
        in Cauchon's rib.
I'll score it on my margin.   You shall see
He'll never air his English for a week.

BEAUPERE.   You tell it all too barely.   Was the
        hair
Long, which he wore, and loose?

JOAN.   I cannot say.

BEAUPERE. Well then, what fashion was he
clothed?

JOAN.   Nor that.

BEAUPERE. Not that! Then, haply, was he
clothed at all?

VOICE. For shame!

ANOTHER.   A villain question!

JOAN.   Do you think
God cannot clothe His Angels if He will?

VOICE. Well spoken, Joan.

ANOTHER.   The Doctor has it.

CAUCHON (*angrily*).   Sirs,
I will have silence. Usher, note me you
If any break it.

BEAUPERE (*continuing*). Was it Michael then
Who brought your King the sign at Chinon?

JOAN.   No.

BEAUPERE. Who then?

JOAN.   I will not answer of the sign.

BEAUPERE. Nay, but you must.

JOAN.   If I should burn for it,
And here the doomsman stood to bear me off,
Nay, tho' he set his torch against the brands,
I would not answer what concerns my King.

ISAMBARD. I pray you, my Lord Bishop, press it not.
She may in right refuse it.

CAUCHON.   I may waive
This question, pending counsel. Pass we on.

    BEAUPERE.   You swore to answer all that touched
       the faith.
Then must you answer this: what doctrine ever
Imparts this Michael?

    JOAN.   But how mean you, sir?

    BEAUPERE.   The Holy Ones should bring us truth,
       then he—
What teaches Michael?

    JOAN.   O, a holy truth!
He taught me sorrow for our woeful France;
Sorrow and love for France. He said to me,
'Be good and true, and where God sends you, go;
Fear not; such pity upon France has He.'
His voice was like all music as he spoke,
And like a river it uplifted me,
To bear me where he willed. I would that you,
You all could hear it; you would pity then,
O surely, the dear land and love her, you,
Not trouble her with wars. See, here is Joan
Bound, and she cannot battle any more,
Only beseech you by the love of Christ
To love as He doth.

    CAUCHON.   Shut her mouth; no more!
Notaries there!

    COLLES.   My lord.

CAUCHON. *Omittite:*

Non tangit hoc processum.

MANCHON (*aside*). Touches not
The trial! Doth it not? It touches me,
God wot, and shrewdly.

JOAN (*pointing*). See, you make them write
What harms me; things that help, you leave un-
> writ.
You sit to judge me here and are not just.
. . . Ah! there will be deliverance.

CAUCHON. Say you so?
Your Voices promise this? . . . But answer me;
It is my question—

JOAN. Does it touch my trial?

CAUCHON. How not? It is your Voices that we
> judge.

JOAN. Why, see then that they judge not you.
> They said,
'You shall be freed by a great victory, Joan;
Be fearless and of cheer.'

CAUCHON. How read you that?

JOAN. I know not if yourselves will set me free,
Or God will break my prison. One of these.

DE FONTE. Troth, Joan, you need not lie so long
> in ward.
There is a better way.

JOAN. Nay, tell me that.

De Fonte. That you submit yourself, your words
and deeds,
To Holy Church.

Joan.   O but how gladly will I !
For when have I done other?   Deed and word
God and the Saints have taught me every one.

De Fonte. You have not understood; I said
'the Church.'

Joan. God and the Church, it is all one for
us.

Manchon (*aside*). Poor child, to think it.

De Fonte.   Joan, you have to know
There is the Church in heaven, the saints with God,
But here on earth is the Church Militant,
I mean the Pope and bishops and the priests,
And all good Christian folk.   When these are met
Duly, God's Spirit guides; they cannot err.

Joan (*aside*). These are the bishops and the
priests.   O Christ !
(*Aloud*) I will submit me to the Church of God.

Cauchon. To the Church Militant.

Joan (*holding up her hand toward secretaries*).   I
said not that.

Cauchon. You shall submit you to the Church
on earth.

Isambard. Joan, to the Pope refer your cause,
the Pope.

JOAN. Kind sir; yes, yes, let the Pope try it, he
Will judge aright.

CAUCHON. The Pope is far to seek.
The Holy Office is the Pope in France.
I marvel, Friar, you dare, unasked of me,
To counsel with the accused. Be warned. Again,
Joan, will you yield you to the Church or no?

JOAN. I told you I would yield to Holy
Church.

CAUCHON. Why, then, to the Church Militant.

JOAN. I said
The Holy Church. It is the Church in heaven,
Christ, and the Virgin, and the blessed Saints,
And the pure Angels.

CAUCHON. This is not to yield.
Once more I warn you mend your answer, girl.

JOAN. I will not answer other. It is said.
(*Buries her face a moment, then raising
her hand.*)
It is enough. O send me back again
To God, who sent me hither.
Here have I nothing more to do, no more;
Why should I tarry? Send me whence I came.
(*A silence in the Hall.*)

CAUCHON. Take her again to cell. The court
will rise.
Henceforth we need attendance but of those

Whom I shall cite expressly; all the rest
I leave to their affairs unburdened.

(*They begin to go out.*)

MANCHON (*putting up his writing*).   Ay,
The dark, the dark! and, soft, we're off a-mousing!

SCENE II.—THE PRISON OF JOAN.   EARLY
MORNING

JOAN *lying on her bed.   A* SOLDIER *on guard*

SOLDIER.   Joan, I have good news for you this morning.

JOAN.   O tell me.

SOLDIER.   You shall have company again.

JOAN.   What company, then?

SOLDIER.   His that was here on Thursday for two hours, and before that on Monday, the Lorrainer prisoner.   How!   Hast no thanks for that?   'Tis kind in the Captain to send a countryman here to cheer you.

JOAN.   It is kind in him.   (*Aside*) But the man cheers me not: I am right sorry for his case, but I cannot like him.

SOLDIER.   He will come in no long time.   Want you aught?   We will leave you for the while.

. JOAN. Ah! friend, I thank you for that.

SOLDIER (*aside*). Poor wench, she may that.
Some of my mates here are ill mates for her, God
forgive 'em. But if she could smell out the devil
under the gaol frock of him that we bring her, she'd
like our company better. (*Goes.*)

JOAN (*sitting up on her bed*). Weary, how weary
am I. Yet I slept

Long, if a sleep it was indeed, and not
A vigil of shut lids. 'Art thou so sure?
Sure?' it went knelling like a woe-bell, 'sure?'
All the night through. And I am weak in sleep,
I could not dumb it. Can I dumb it now?
They are all learned, they say they are the Church.
The Church is Christ and Mary and the Saints,
Michael, and Margaret, and Catherine.
They do not speak like this Church Militant,
But counter to it; and they look, ah me!
How otherwise! kind eyes and true that gaze
Right down in my heart, like stars that look
Into the clear deep of a little well.
But those men's eyes are hard: they smite on me
Yet never enter in my heart at all
And see within it. O if they would see
God's message written there so plain, so plain,
They would not call me rebel to the Church.
Why will they call me rebel? When have I

Been rebel to the Voices? save indeed
For the mad leap from Beaurevoir.   (I thought
They'd slaughter the poor babes of Compiègne,
If they broke in by lack of Joan : the Saints,
Though they forbade, I thought would bear me up.)
No, no, I am faithful daughter of the Church,
The holy Church, the Church that is in heaven,
The Church that is within me, yea, within :
Ah ! blessed Lord, within.

      .   .   .   .   .

Yet ' Art thou sure ? '   Joan shall be freed, they said,
By a great victory : very clear they said it.
And I twelve dreadful moons a prisoner !
Christ, if they cannot do it—.
For still they come, ah me ! but paler now,
As in a cloud ; and still they speak, but dumb
As one that hails a drowner under wave.
If they should cease ; if these great doctors spake
Truth, when they called them dreams !   O God my life,
I stretch my arms to find Thee : will the earth
Stagger and crumble under, drop me down
Out of Thine hand, out of Thine eyes, beyond
Thy knowing, into nothingness ?   O Thou,
Who livest ever, reach a hand and hold.

      .   .   .   .   .

Yea, 'tis the doubts are shadows, not the Saints.
They will deliver.

Enter behind her RAIMOND, *disguised.   He stands a
moment*

RAIMOND.   You give me not good morrow, gentle
dame.

JOAN.   I thought you were that prisoner from
Lorraine :

You are other by the voice.

RAIMOND.   Your ears are true,
As, God be thanked, your keeper's are not.   Maid,
Give wonder not a word, but look.

(*Discovers himself.*)

JOAN.   A friend !
The wonder is too wonderful for word. . . .
But come you here as captive ?

RAIMOND.   Yea and nay.
I pass for that mock-captive whom they bring
To trap your franker speech, and guide the judge
Where he may probe you deftest.   Let him not
Know himself known, yet foil him all you may.
That first.   And then—O have you hope : Xaintrailles
Gathers a force to Beauvais ; when he strikes
'Twill be to clutch some captive of their best
—Yea, Bedford's self, if he ride loosely fenced—
And hold him for your ransom.   Last, if this
Too slowly ripen, here in Rouen are

Four that have made adventure with myself,
By harbourage of secret friends of France,
To spirit you out of ward, or as you pass
From cell to judgment hall.   I came to seek
Guidance for hour and place and shift from you.

    JOAN.   Friend beyond speech, what thanks to
        render !

    RAIMOND.   None :

Or these—to teach us how to steal you forth.

    JOAN.   How shall I ?   Hate has ears and eyes
        and hands

Jealous and quick as love's.   Never a slip,
A doze, a nod, a dally.   You would beat
Your lives out on my cage, not open it.

    RAIMOND.   Our lives out !   Blithely, if the price
        be this.

    JOAN.   Ah ! but to pay the price, yet—.   Tell me
        why

You risk dear life even now to speak with me.
Did the King bid you venture ?

    RAIMOND.   Maid, the King

Does nothing, lacking Joan at side.

    JOAN (*pauses*).   Alas !

But the dear folk of France ?

    RAIMOND.   My tongue is shamed

To tell how they are silent.   Tremouille rides
High like a hawk, and all beneath are stilled.

JOAN (*after a pause*). Then you, why did you
    dare it?

RAIMOND.   Ask me not.

And yet I'll tell. It was the bitter shame
That wrung me on that wall in Compiègne.
I sinned, I too, the traitor-sin, for I,
Trusting the traitors, lost you. All my blood
Poured out in peril, could it wash my veins
Pure of the shame that poisons them?

JOAN.   My friend,
You shall not wrong, even you, the truest heart
That beats in France. A blindness is not sin.
And, if it were, shame would not bring you hither.
Men will not be so brave for only shame.

RAIMOND. Joan, a man could not choose but
    come.

JOAN.   Yet they
Choose, all men, to abide at home, for me.
You have not told me yet.

RAIMOND.   Why, then, I cannot.

JOAN. But, Raimond, Joan can tell it you. The
    day
Is not so far since Raimond told his heart.
That which has risked you here—men call it love.

RAIMOND. You shall not say it; I vowed it should
    not be
Breathed by us here, nor thought. Am I so vile?

All hope of guerdon, like a vice, I slew
First ere I ventured.   Should the Maid of France
Buy freedom at a price?   Forget your word.
I am not so ill a scholar of the Maid.

    JOAN.   Sweet saints, how wondrous is this love
        of man,
Which yet ye never told me of!   It takes
Men by the hand and leads them up to death,
As if it were that strong love known of us
That taught all deeds of mine.   And yet to me
Strange is it, or—I shudder—a beast of prey
With eyes of hunger tethered near me——

            (*Catches at* RAIMOND *as if in fear.*)
    RAIMOND.   Joan,
You shall not linger in this devils' den.
Is there no God in earth, then?

    JOAN.   Yesterday
I could have asked it, friend: but here this hour
Stand you beside the lonely one, a man,
And in your eyes of man the eternal love
Written.   I know there is a God on earth.
All is well now, yea, though we died to-day.

    RAIMOND.   I can die, Joan, with you: but O not
        here.
Not here, but where the loudest and the last
Of battles hurls those island archers off
The vesture-hems of France: O there we'll end

Among the lightnings, Maid, and holy fire
Of God, as we began it.

JOAN (*to herself*).   Ay, they said,
'By a great victory.' Wherefore is it, I
Cannot believe?

RAIMOND.   Our time is growing short.
Consult how we may steal you.

JOAN.   Peace! He comes.
Stay, I will tell.

SOLDIER *re-enters*

Good keeper, give us yet
One moment's speech before you lead him back.

(JOAN *and* RAIMOND *converse in whispers.*)

SOLDIER (*aside*).   It turns an English stomach
     when they set
Yon knave to trap her thus. The Fowler, ha!
For that's his name by meaning: mighty fit.
He's lured the poor bird to his nets at last,
'Tis easy seen. But I could baulk him yet
Of this last secret. Stay: for all is one.
She must come to it at end: what matter how?
But I like ill to watch it. (*To* RAIMOND) Bide awhile
Longer: I leave you.   (*Goes out.*)

JOAN (*aloud*).   'Tis a chance, no more.

RAIMOND. But we will make it more.

JOAN.   I think not so.

RAIMOND.   You, Joan, to be the doubter !

JOAN.   Other times
I have seen, as in a picture, all my haps.
Joan in her armour again—I see not her.

RAIMOND.   Yea, we'll not risk the Maid in fight,
    but keep
Beyond the shot of malice.   She will send
Her soul beside us into battle.

JOAN.   Yea,
That I can image.   That will be.   But now
Take farewell of me, ere he come again.
Perhaps for all your boasting, we shall take
Never another.

RAIMOND.   Joan, if I have dared
Aught, it was taught me by yourself, and you
To daunt me thus !   It is the prison shades
Darken your spirit.

JOAN.   Is it dark ?   Ah no.
A light is growing in me, while we talk,
Dim, but it pierces.   There's some other way
Of the great victory, Raimond. . . .
This is the price, my soul, it is the price.

RAIMOND.   What mean you ?

JOAN.   That the Maid shall die, because
Without her death there had not been her deed.
Did not those iron hearts of England break
By their own fable that I fought from hell ?

And by that fable must I perish now.
They dared not face me, for they thought me witch;
And, for they think me witch, they dare not spare.

RAIMOND.   What hell is black enough for the lie that links

Hell's name with thine?

JOAN.   My foes have cause to hate.
My countrymen, what do they?

RAIMOND.   Spare us, Joan.
'Not all forget thee.

JOAN.   See, again, the price.
I saved them by the name of Heaven: how else
Had the French heart gone with me up the walls?
Our counsellors love not the name of Heaven;
Had saved me, were't an earthlier.   'Tis the price.

RAIMOND.   O you have paid that price a hundred times

Already in this horror; you have been
Martyr of France enough.   You shall not die
For fancies.   Maid, it is an idle thing
I plead (you gave it speech; I shamed to do it),
Yet by the love that is come here to die
If death could win the Maiden's life, O yet
Be brave to live; let not my love be vain.

JOAN (*taking his two hands*).   Can love be vain?
O, then, of friends the first
And last of all, believer to the end,

N

Listen.　They call me on the tongues of men
The Maid: those Others have another name,
'Daughter of God': they ever hail me so;
'Daughter of God.'　Then in my Father's house
Shall I be given in marriage, by His hand,
Or howsoe'er the just are joined in one.
Who knoweth, Raimond, that thy love was vain?
. . . I hear the step that parts us.　Guard you heaven
Safe hence from their espial!　Nay, no word.

> (RAIMOND *kisses her hand.　The door
> opens, and he goes away with the*
> SOLDIER.)

> JOAN (*turned towards the door, listening*).　Down
> . . . down . . . the foot goes down the
> tower, and out:

Out of my life.　Last of my friends.　Had I
So spoken, if I be to speak again
On this side of the door of death?　Ah! no.
There's no man will deliver Joan.

> (*Low music.　The room softly illumined.*)
> Who spake?
> (*Turns.*)

Who? . . . For thou art not Michael of the sword.
I know thee not. . . . And yet I fear thee not,
Being so gentle.
Nay, by the maiden lily, art thou he
That hailed the maiden-mother?

O holy and O tender, if thou hast
For me some word of comfort, even me,
Speak comfort, tell me what shall be the end.

(Kneels.)

Deliverance? Those others promise it
So oft, yet am I not delivered. . . . Ah!
Shall I be that, and surely? Bear me then
Thither, O brother of the skies. . . . Alas,
Not yet? What have I more to work on earth?
. . . To suffer? Is not this to suffer? See,
The chain, the lonely dark, those hungry eyes.
. . . How say'st? It must be by the fire? Not that!
Ah, no, no, no, not that! 'Twere easier die
Seven times by steel in battle than by fire.
This virgin and untainted flesh of mine,
What hath it done that it must burn to ash?
O seraph of the tenderness of God,
Pity me, pray the kind God ask not that.

(Lies prostrate: then rises to her knees.)

Ah, what is this? Over me went his wing,
Flame, and it slew not. O, it wrapped me round
With the embrace of God: it leaves my heart
Flaming; it slays in it the fear. Behold
The handmaid of the Lord. I'll come to thee,
Yea, thro' the fire, great brother, thro' the fire.

SCENE III.—Sully.   A Room.

Tremouille *and* Regnault

Regnault.   And have you further news of her ?
Tremouille.   Ah ! no ;
But shall have.
Regnault.   And your forecast of the event ?
Tremouille.   Like all the world's—her death.
Regnault.   A cruel end.
Tremouille.   You thought not to advise De
    Flavy so,
In time.
Regnault.   How mean you that ?
Tremouille.   O be discreet :
We name it not between us.   Yet I ask,
Have you foreseen the sequel, if the girl,
Seeing the faggot near, should—speak at last ?
Regnault.   What should she speak ?
Tremouille.   The thing we do not name
Between us.   It may touch your honour, friend.
Regnault.   Mine !   You were with me.
Tremouille.   You misspelt, I say,
My letter.   Read, and own it so.   Besides,
There's a broad letter that denounces her,
Yours, on her capture.   O, the folk are dumb,

Not dullard: they will bring their murdered saint
To lay her down at her Archbishop's door.

    REGNAULT.   La Tremouille, what would you goad
       me to?

    TREMOUILLE.   Could you not buy her—for a
       nunnery?

    REGNAULT. Why that?

    TREMOUILLE.   The silence.

    REGNAULT.   Ha! . . . but will they sell?

    TREMOUILLE. You go to market late; but, as I
       hear,

The Church is claimant for her. Help the Church
To bury her—unburnt.

    REGNAULT.   The English?

    TREMOUILLE.   Yes,

It baulks them of the bonfire. Then the price
Must 'quite them. O, you will not grudge the cost
For the Archbishop's name and sanctities.
But lose no hour: it hangs in dainty poise,
As say my agents.

    REGNAULT.   It shall go to hand.
And yet it will not speed. (*Is going, but turns.*) O
     Tremouille,
Why did you hate her so?

    TREMOUILLE.   And why again,
Regnault, will you miscall a coldness, hate?
I am no priest: the Saints are none of mine.

Regnault. (*aside*).   Had I but seen her face at
    Compiègne
Before—O God !   (*Goes.*)
Tremouille.   It will not speed—with *him*.
                  (*Moves to the fireside.*)
It is the very curse of villainy
You cannot ease heart-sickness on the ear
Even of your brother-villain, even his :
Nay, tho' your brother-villain be the priest.
 . . . There was a woman burnt when I was
    young.
I saw the fire upspurt, I heard her shriek.
God's death ! it tore my bowels.   And to me
The wretch was nought ; I had no hand in it.
 . . . Yonder's the chair she sat in, and my child
Upon her lap : the imp, he pulled her down,
Kissed her, and laughing round upon me, cries,
' Father, you cannot love the Maiden Joan
As baby George can love her.'—Cursèd chance
That brought her meddling hither !

             Enter Raimond

                  Ah ! so soon !
You will be wearied with the journey, sir.
Doubtless your news will wait.
    Raimond.   If Death would wait.
If you are minded help her, move at once.

TREMOUILLE (*aside*).   Rude, on my faith.   But
　　　can I spare him yet?
(*Aloud*) How I am minded, sir, my messenger,
Who brought you back, instructs you.   But the means
Are in dispute.   Your counsel.

RAIMOND.　　　　　　　　　　　Fight for her,
And treat; the twain together.   Troops afield
Will weight the scale of ransom till it sinks,
And lifts Joan out of prison.

TREMOUILLE.　　　　　　　　Eloquent,
Even in your ruffled moments!   Your advice
Is spark to tinder.   I had planned the march
Of strong battalions to the Beauvais camp.

RAIMOND.   And will they come?

TREMOUILLE.　　　　　　　　　I said it.

RAIMOND.　　　　　　　　　　Pardon me;
'Planned' was your word.   It is a year too late
For planning; and the days are scant to do.

TREMOUILLE.   The trial draws to close, then?

RAIMOND.　　　　　　　　　Hour by hour
Expect it.

TREMOUILLE.   But she makes a stout defence.
The King—how fares it with his credit there?

RAIMOND.   She speaks no word to his dishonour,
　　　nay,
Nor lets be spoken.

TREMOUILLE.　　　And the Council? . . . Ah,

We know our helplessness may seem neglect,
Yet—

RAIMOND.　　Of the Council she has said no word

TREMOUILLE.　None ?

RAIMOND.　　　She has hope they will deliver her.

TREMOUILLE (*after a moment's pause*).　Sir, I shall
　　　post this warrant for the march
While you are resting.

RAIMOND.　　　　　　I return this hour.

TREMOUILLE.　It will outrun you northward.
　　　Speed you well.　　　　　　(RAIMOND *goes.*)
The hound !　And I must brook his insolence,
As if 'twere fawning.　When the hunt is done,
The lash for him.　(*Goes to table and begins to write.*)
　　　　　These musters, then.　He spoke
Good sense enough : the troops afield will help
Our paltering Regnault, if——　　　(*Stops the pen.*)
　　　　　　The folly of it !
Wilt write thy power's death-warrant, then ?　The host
That saves, reseats.　Joan with the King again !
Joan and La Tremouille beside him !　No.
I cannot look upon the face of her
Now.　(*Throws down the pen.*)　God in Heaven,
　　　some other way of it !　　(*Buries his face.*)
Good Angels, keep her silent to the end !

SCENE IV.—A Kitchen in Rouen

Jacques *and* Minstrel *seated*

Minstrel *sings*

Flutter and beat on thy bars, O dove,
  Child of the field and the sky !
Beat, or brood in the dark thereof,
  Listing if Death draw nigh.
Wings to hover and bless were thine ;
  But where is the wing to flee ?
O White Dove of the Pity divine,
  And who hath pity of thee ?

Jacques. No more, Minstrel, no more !   Have not you and I pity of her, and two more ?   'Tis nigh as many as stuck to her by the ditch of St. Pierre.

Minstrel. O you were there, Jacques.   Tell me again.

Jacques. They had run and left her, the rest of them.   Then comes D'Aulon, lol-lolloping up (he'd thrown his crutches down to climb a-horseback) and croaked out, 'What was she doing there all alone ?' Then she upped visor and answered him, ' Nay, friend, for I have fifty thousand here '; and while he was dazing round to count us (six we were all told, till an arrow knocked young Andrè out of the reckoning) she sang out, 'Ho there! to the faggots, every one!' and, Lord's my life! they came swarming out of cover again as if she had shaken a hive, and filled the ditch up, and went over, and in, before the Godons could loose three shots from the mangonel. Minstrel, when we were through, I sat and clutched a battlement to steady my whirls: I was clean drunk with the pure wonder of it. Heyday! Yet I would the Scot were home from Beauvais.

MINSTREL. He is in the street.

JACQUES. How? Canst hear him?

MINSTREL. Not yet; but he is nigh.

JACQUES. Thou hast a touch of *her* gift, like the Scot. Sooth, I can prophesy now, for I know that footfall.

Enter the SCOT

(*Aside*) Glum enough! He has not sped. (*Aloud*) Your news is bad.

SCOT. Ah! So ye ken that! Well, the worse the news, the more need to wet lip first. I have not eaten these twelve hours.

(MINSTREL *gets him food.*)

JACQUES. But are they coming? Ay or No?

SCOT. Let a man be. (*Begins to eat.*) But I can listen. How goes it with her?

JACQUES. Very nigh killing, last Thursday. They
had her abroad on a stage, and all the reverend doctors
and the English Cardinal on another; and Brother
Erard preached her his best for half an hour by the
market-clock. Lord, but she spoilt his chant once!

SCOT. Ay, how?

JACQUES. Why he was running up the scale about
the 'noble house of France,' and what shame it was
it should be abused by the heretic woman, and how
the King was become a heretic by her, when there
broke in that clear voice of hers with the child-music
in it, that I thought never to hear again: 'By my
faith, sir, and I say it on pain of my life, he is the
most Christian of all Christian men.'

SCOT. Ah! that was Joan! What did Erard?

JACQUES. Bit at her and bawled like a parrot to
'shut her mouth.' It was too late; she had cracked
his trumpet for him, and the folk were jogging one
another's sides and laughing under their palms.
Then the reverend sirs began to get restive, the
Cardinal's folk cursing the Bishop, and he spitting
back, till I whispered old Pierre, 'Three minutes more
of this, and we shall see these grand sirs tearing their
collars between them.' The folk began to bustle too,
and a stone or so came off the crowd and rattled on
the scaffold-poles over Cauchon. I take it 'twas the
English cast them.

Scot.   Nay, they had made better shooting; 'twas your own folk, Jacques.   And then?

Jacques.   Why, then the doctors fell together again by falling all upon Joan, and they so belaboured her with shouts and threats to unsay her saints and voices, that at last—well, anyway she's alive yet and safe.

Scot.   Ah! what said she?

Jacques.   There was old Fire-the-faggot in his death-cart under the scaffold ready to take her off and burn her, except she abjured.   St. Nod, he was as bleached as his own wood ashes, and shook as if it was himself must ride the back seat, not she.   Then Massieu, that keeps her on the Court days, prayed her for the love of God to say Ay.   So she nodded; and a clerk of the Cardinal's whipped a slip of parchment out of his sleeve the size of a batten, and she spoke the words after him that read it, and then marked it with a pen.   She smiled all the while, and some cried she was but mocking them, but it seemed to me she was in a dream, like my Catharine, when she walked in her sleep, and I stayed her at the window-sill.

Scot.   But she lives, she lives?

Jacques.   Yes, they had her back to——

Scot (*springing up*).   God's mercy!   Then she shall live to unsay the unsaying of it.

Jacques.   What's this, man?

SCOT.   It's Xaintrailles and seven thousand stout fellows behind him knocking at the prison-door this day se'nnight.

JACQUES.   St. Thunder! and you ate your supper and never told us.

SCOT.   You told my news before me, did ye not? And could I speak it myself till I knew it was worth the telling?   But he's coming, friends, he's coming, and Monday night next you and I will slip the bolt to him.

JACQUES (*embracing him*).   God love you, God love you, for the best Frenchman in broad France.   Tell us it all.

SCOT.   Ay, when ye give me the breath back: I'm ill at your foreign beloverings.   I say Xaintrailles will be seven thousand strong at the week end, and he is to make a night march in her old style on Monday: and if we four, with a friend or two, cannot cut up a postern's guard when they whistle us outside, and man the gate for King Charles and the Maid, then we be grown rusty with hiding.   Hey! to think I may have my shot yet at Brown Robin!

MINSTREL (*murmuring*).   'O a maid shall have might on the arrow, the arrow.'

JACQUES.   Go on, Scot; don't stay for him.

SCOT.   One thing I like ill.   There's with them in camp the doited creature of a prophet they picked off a sheep run ; says 'God sent him in place of Joan, for she was so proud.' God send him further, say I. He is like her as apes be to men, or polecats to lions.

(*He draws out a picture from his breast and looks at it.*)

JACQUES. What hast there ?

SCOT. Her likeness is it ; I had it from a clansman. He made it at Rheims, and gave it me when he died coming back from Noyon bridge. Look there ! and they to go after that blear-eyed sheep's head with his mouth ajar !

JACQUES. Let him serve till she's a-horseback. Here's to Charles and the Maid ! Charles and the Maid !   (*Drinks.*)

Enter RAIMOND

Drink, sir, drink to the Maid. They are here in a week.

RAIMOND. A week !

JACQUES. What ails you, sir, to look that-wise ?

RAIMOND. A day were too late, now.

JACQUES. Love o' God ! How is that ?

RAIMOND. They will do her to death to-morrow.

JACQUES. Nay, they gave her her life for unsaying her visions.

RAIMOND. She hath unsaid it back again. And, more, they found her in man's dress again, and that is heresy, saith the Bishop. God's curse on these devils in gowns! (*Fiercely*) Scot!

SCOT (*turning to him*). Ay.

RAIMOND. Thou said'st thou would'st go with me after her to death's door.

SCOT. I'll go that far.

RAIMOND. We must go farther, belike — and thro' it.

SCOT. Small's my care for the soldier trade, if she be out of it. I'll not stint you, sir.

JACQUES. Nor I.

MINSTREL. Nor I.

RAIMOND. Then listen. They must bring her past Pierre's doorway here, and this is the very warren of Rouen. Once past the door and thro' a passage or two, there's a week's hiding here. The Minstrel and Jacques shall wait here in the doorway, while the Scot and I snatch her from the cart. They will let me near the wheels to speak with her, for I will wear the gear I played Loiseleur with. Then when I lift her, strike you in right and left, Scot, while I give her to the Minstrel and Jacques keeps the door. Then, afterwards, fall it as it may fall.

SCOT. 'Tis likeliest *we* shall fall. But we'll die for her before she shall die for France.

RAIMOND. There's a hope, friends, yet. There is a hope.

SCENE V.—Outside the Gate of Prison

*Crowd of poor men and women, with candles, praying
and chanting the ' Miserere.'* RAIMOND *and* SCOT
standing near.

FIRST WOMAN.   Canst hear, if they be chanting
      yet ?   I think
'Tis ended.

SECOND WOMAN.   Never Mass again for Joan,
Saving they say it yonder with the Saints.

FIRST WOMAN.   Is she not damned for heresy?

SECOND WOMAN.   You to say it
That have a daughter !   Damned ? the child that
      took
Clothing of man to keep her maidenhood.
The martyr of all maids, say I.

THIRD WOMAN.   But say it
Low, gossip, lest the soldiers hear you.   See,
The death-cart.   Lord have pity on her soul.

Enter SOLDIERS, *and take up stand at gate*

(RAIMOND, *disguised as in Scene II.,
      approaches one of them.*)

RAIMOND.   Art he they call Brown Robin ?

SOLDIER.   If it were,
Sirrah, your right to ask.   What call they you?

RAIMOND.   Nay, but you know me well.

SOLDIER.   And over well :
There's no such plenty of the rascal breed.

RAIMOND.   Who then?

SOLDIER.   The Bishop's terrier, that he slips
Into her earth to draw her. . Dirty dogs
For dirty work.   We hunt with foreigners;
There's never English kind will do it.

RAIMOND.   At least,
You know me.

SOLDIER.   Sooth, and small's the pleasure o't.

RAIMOND.   Were it more pleasure know my gold?

SOLDIER.   O ay,
Monk, if it be less counterfeit than thou.

RAIMOND.   Be you but honest as these crowns,
          and I   (*Showing money.*)
Will better them at night.

SOLDIER (*takes the money*),   Say on.

RAIMOND.   Let me cross speech with her beside
          the wheels,
And close : the thing is secret.

SOLDIER.   , An I may.
Stand off.   I hear them on the stair.

RAIMOND.   But do it.
                              (*Exit.*)

o

PRIESTS *come out from gate, chanting*

Lord of ruth and loving-kindness,
Over sinner in his blindness,
　Heed Thy child and shrive.
Out of error and misdoing,
Unto wisdom, unto rueing,
　Save her soul alive.

God, that in Thy furnace wholly
Changest hearts of men by holy
　Breath of purging fire.
Her by mortal pains deliver,
And forbid she bear for ever
　Heaven's immortal ire.

(JOAN *comes in sight.*)

THIRD WOMAN.　Look where she comes.　Nay,
　nay, they will not dare
To burn that meek white angel.

FIRST WOMAN.　　　　　Comfort her,
Comfort her, holy Jesu.

SECOND WOMAN.　　Shame !　I'll say it :
Shame on you, murderers all ; how dare ye do it ?

VOICES.　Shame on the English !　Shame on
　Cauchon !

ROBIN (*threatening*).　　　　　How ?

French dogs, ye dare to yap, then.   Must ye learn
Your masters by the sting of quarter-staff?

JOAN.   Ah! do not strike them.   Am I not enough
To die for this?   These cannot hurt you, they.

(To the people.)

Mothers and maids of Rouen, pray for Joan
That Christ be near her in the bitter pain :
As I will pray Him that He visit never
This murder on your babes.

ROBIN.   Set forward, ho !
Fellows, her prating will make broken heads.

(SOLDIERS lead JOAN to the cart.   PRIESTS
follow, chanting.)

RAIMOND and SCOT re-enter behind

RAIMOND.   Four paces to the rear of me; but then
Close up, a lance-length from the doorstep.

SCOT.   Ay !

RAIMOND.   'Tis our life, Kenneth, tho' we win her.

SCOT.   Ay !
Sir, I had reckoned.

RAIMOND.   Then for France and her
Come after !

A SOLDIER (stopping them).   Stay awhile ; there's
    throng enow
I' the roadway, fellows !

Scot (*tripping him*).   Nay, there's room i' the
road
Enough to measure with thine inches.

(*To* Raimond.)
Quick,

Sir, ere they note us!

Soldier.   Villainy!   Stay them, ho!

> (Raimond *and* Scot *rush off.   Noise of
> a struggle, and they reappear, attacked
> by* Soldiers. *The* Scot *is driven,
> fighting, up a side street.* Raimond *is
> engaged by* Brown Robin, *whom he
> has wounded.*)

Brown Robin.   Thou'lt render for that scratch,
fool youngster!   There,

(*Runs him through.*)

Wilt break the peace no more in Rouen!   Now,
His fellow; Rob it is shall have the brace.

(*Exit in pursuit of* Scot.)

SCENE VI.—A Street near the Market-place
of Rouen

Raimond *seated on the ground.   The* Scot *enters*

Scot.   Alone, and hurt—and Jacques not with
you!

RAIMOND.   Nay,
They had me home and tended. They are gone
To watch—ah! God. I could not bide, I dragged
My body thus far. Friend, I thought you slain.

SCOT. I kept my guard up till I found a door
And shut the dogs out. They were whistled off.
Mayhap, my skin was little worth the hunt;
So they went growling back. There's one of them
Goes home feet foremost; O but light's my heart
That I have paid Brown Robin.

RAIMOND.   Where's the use?
Scot, will she die the lighter for't? Alas,
We talk and she is dying. Come away—

                                    (*Tries to rise.*)

SCOT. Come can ye not, unless I carry you;
And that I will not.

RAIMOND.   Do you fear them so?
I thought you hardier, friend.

SCOT.   For hardihood,
I find it as I need; but not for this.
Sir, I can look on death, if't be my own;
Look upon hers I cannot.

RAIMOND.   Speed me then,
Heaven! Since I could not help her with a blow,
Cannot I win to help her with a prayer?

SCOT. Couldst not look on and live.

RAIMOND.   Why, do I not

Look on it, here? O, Scot, I see it all;
It eats my flesh like fire to see it. O think;
There's our white lamb before her slaughterers dumb.
A black-fleeced gownsman of their Satan's-fold
Preaches the leering crowd her devilries,—
Hers! And no face of friend to cast the lie
Back again. Up, I'll reach her, if I crawl!

                       (*Tries to move and stays.*)

I bleed within; I cannot come to thee.

    SCOT (*supporting his head*). I fear me lest he crawl
        too soon across
Doom-threshold.

    RAIMOND. Ah! he's done. They'll let her
        pray
A little minute. Joan, I had no prayer
That time. . . . But there's St. Michael and His
        sword,
Look, on the wall . . . so, let us kneel together;
I'll pray him smite but once. . . . *His* sword was
        never
Broken. . . .

    SCOT. Is light of head: the happier he.
Christ, if I too could overdream this horror
And wake to learn her flitted!

    RAIMOND. Ho! the wolves!
The wolves, look, in a circle, staring at her,
The babe . . . they grow so plenty by the wars . . .

A brand, a brand, a brand to cast at them.
Quick, ere they sink fang in her.   How they gnarr!
SCOT.   The fever grows upon him.   O the boy
That I so loved—after herself.

RAIMOND.   Off, off!
Will no one shut the gate upon the pack?
Here's one will shut it; he's the King o' the wolves.
Nay, but thou'rt liker fox, so velvet-footed,
And ermine-throated as a chancellor.
Sir, I am sure you do not mean her harm;
Give me her back. . . .
Steady, Rolande; she's coming soon afield. . . .
What say'st?   Without?   Villain, to shut her out,
And all the hell-dogs round her!   The red tongues
Lick out at her, they shoot like leaping flames.
Why, why, 'tis fire indeed: it wilts her flesh.
She cannot bear to burn, she is but girl;
Have mercy—
Those maiden limbs to ash!   How dare ye?
SCOT.   Cease.
This dream is worse than waking.

RAIMOND (*collecting himself*).   Ah! the Scot.
Is it so late?   We'll buckle sword. . . . Alas,
It was a dream, and she has yet to die.
Hush! canst not hear the chain grate as they gird
That white virginity to the felon stake?
Horrible, horrible.   And one sets a torch,

And up, up, up, the wicked hungering flame
Dances and leaps and strikes not, leaps again
And dallies out the torment. God in heaven,
How couldst thou make this maiden and those men?

 Scot. Peace, sir, for pity.

 Raimond.   Hark, it roars on her,
It wraps her round with agony. Tender skies,
Are ye grown hard and have no rains in you
To dout this furnace heat of hell? The air
All is a-tremble with it and a-scorch
To where we sit and shudder. Christ, I cannot
Brook even the throb and fume of it, and she—

 Scot. Peace, ere you mad us both. Perhaps,
  who knows?
They would not burn her, only scare again
To call her voice a liar.

 Raimond.   Forbear, forbear.
Scot, you have stabbed me deeper than my wound.
If she belie it, there's no God in heaven,
Nor no truth under heaven. Away, away.
It is the fire of God that comes between,
       (*Struggles to his feet.*)
But I'll come to thee through it. . . . Ah!

 Scot.   What is't?

 Raimond (*his head drooping*). A string broke at
  my heart. The Maid is sped.
    (*The* Scot *lets him sink to the ground.*)

SCOT (*aside*). I think it be so verily.

> (*Drawing out the portrait and kissing it.*)
>
> This was she.

What like, I wonder, is she now?

RAIMOND (*gazing before him*). Yea, like!

Is she not like? And yet—

SCOT (*following his eyes*). Why gaze you there?

RAIMOND. Can you not see her, then, and she so
> near?

. . . The fire has changed thy robes, and yet I know
> not

If man's they be or woman's.

SCOT. Dreaming still.

RAIMOND. . . . Brighter than ever armour. 'Tis
> the Saints

Have clad their sister. . . . Smiling under tears,

As after Patay field.

SCOT. He sees her sure;

The death-wraith is it that salutes the quick

At parting. God! She'll beckon him away.

What friend has now Scot Kenneth?

> (*To* MINSTREL, *who enters hastily and*
> *would pass them.*)
>
> Stay you, there.

MINSTREL. I cannot stay: I am a wind, a wind;

I wander under heaven to echo it—

The arrow, the arrow, the Maid has trodden it down.

Scot. What sayest, man, what sayest? Hast thou
　　seen?
Minstrel. I saw hell open and her fires a-
　　roar,
And one white angel dumb them.
　　Scot. 　　　　　　　　　　Sober thee;
Speak a plain tale.
　　Minstrel. 　　　　I cannot sober me;
I have drunk the wines of terror and the wines
Of transport in one cup.
　　Scot. 　　　　　　Then, as thou canst.
　　Minstrel. Thousand by thousand on the mortal
　　field,
And she but one. O ho! to war she rides,
Fenceless she rides and single to that war,
Yet shall they not o'erthrow her, a host to one.

They bend their weapons on her and their brows;
They bark like dogs, they gape like dogs to snatch
The soul's betrayal from the shaken lip.
The truth sits in the bosom of a girl,
And who shall storm it thence?

A flood of faces billowing to the walls,
And roofs alive with men. I saw the light
Flit from her lonely eyes to range the flood,
And back return, unrested. And a moan

Came trembling down — the dove's note on the
      bough
When stolen her brood is—crying, 'Rouen, Rouen,
My death be not thy doom !'

The founts of hell upbrake from underneath
And spouted flame to swallow her ; the red surge
Roared up her to the lips.   I heard the hiss   .
Of monsters in the fiery drift, the bruit
Of devil laughter-claps, and hurtling wings
That ploughed the reek about her.

Then from the furnace heart a cry went out,
Scarce louder than a sob, but shook the ranks
With mastery like a trumpet, 'God, my life,
The voice was thine, the voice was thine, the voice
Hath not betrayed me.'   And the cry went out,
And beats on all the walls of all the world,
And none will silence it for evermore.

   RAIMOND. 'With a great victory.'   Saints, ye
       spake her true !
   SCOT.   How brooked her slayers such an end ?
       say on.
   MINSTREL.   As those who smote the breast on
       Calvary, they,—
With eyes that faded in the ruthless laugh,
With blasphemies in hollow silence dead,

With huddled shoulders and hid brows of shame,
And sobbings of the proud, and tempest tears,
And boding rumours that forerun the doom
Ere a lost army sunders.　Lost are they.
France and the Maid !　The Maid hath died for
　　France.
　　RAIMOND.　Hath she but that?　Nay, Minstrel,
　　　　that do I.
For France she lives who made such ending.
　　MINSTREL.　　　　　　　　　　　　　　Yea,
Lives.　Then ye knew it !　Brothers, from the
　　flame
Outhovered, from between the virgin lips,
After the crying of the mortal cry,
A snowy dove, alive, unstained of fire,
And forth it went to range the world.　She lives,
O brothers, yet, and leads us—

　　　　　　JACQUES *and* ISAMBARD *enter*

　　RAIMOND.　　　　　　　　　　Me she leads
Some other whither.　Fetch me here a priest.
　　SCOT.　Here is one now beside you.
　　JACQUES.　　　　　　　　　　This is that
Good Father, who was brave for her in court
And prison, and held up the blessed cross
Beside the fire to help her die.

RAIMOND.   Then who
Like him? He'll know the way she went, and speed
Raimond to find her.

ISAMBARD.   Peace with thee, my son.
            (*Kneels by him. The* MINSTREL *moves
            apart and sings.*)

Saw ye there? a wonder flown from red heart of the
    •   burning.
        Bird is that, or flying brightness?
Nay, from death her Maiden self on silver plume
        returning,
        Lo! of chain and pain unholden,
        Lo! with dove-wing and dove-whiteness
            Shines arrayed.
        France, by her that could not die,
        By the ghostly battle-cry
        Of the truth that would not lie,—
        Follow, where thy banner moves,
        And its white wings are the dove's,
        And again to battle golden
            Rides the Maid.

ISAMBARD.   Good Scot, he beckons you.
SCOT.   What would you, sir?
RAIMOND.   I am the seed of gentlemen of France,
And you a bowman from a Scottish glen;

But of one sister are we brothers both.
Close you my eyes, true brother ; they have seen
Earth's best ; what should they more ?   (*Dies.*)
    Scot.   Has followed her.
                                    (*Kisses his brow.*)
Pass, gentle brother ; and among the Saints
Go tell the Maid that true to her were we.

THE END

Printed by R. & R. Clark, Limited, *Edinburgh*

COLUMBA. [BLACKWOOD]

PRESS NOTICES.

'In *Columba* the Warden of Glenalmond has produced a drama, or rather a dramatic poem, of great insight and beauty.'—*Guardian.*

'Lovers of poetry will certainly find in the attractive volume entitled *Columba, a Drama*, matter to reward a careful reading. . . . To have dealt poetically with a theme which might in weak hands have easily become more pious than poetic, shows a considerable mastery over the conditions of artistic creation.—*Daily Telegraph.*

'Mr. Skrine has in *Columba* made an artistic addition to British literature, though hardly to the British drama.'—*Dramatic Review.*

'We shall venture to say that there is not a weak or unmeaning line in this work, so far as we have observed, from end to end.'—*Educational Review.*

'Mr. Skrine has achieved a work of considerable literary as well as dramatic merit, which should enhance his reputation.'—*Oxford Review.*

'What strikes us most is the calm movement of the lines; Mr. Skrine does what is rarely done—writes blank verse with a note of his own.'—*Speaker.*

BY THE SAME AUTHOR.

A Memory of Edward Thring. By the Rev. JOHN HUNTLEY SKRINE, M.A., Warden of Trinity College, Glenalmond. With a Portrait. Crown 8vo. 6s.

Virgil.—P. Vergili Maronis Georgicon. Liber secundus. Edited for the use of schools by the Rev. JOHN HUNTLEY SKRINE, M.A., Warden of Trinity College, Glenalmond, late Fellow of Merton College, Oxford. Pott 8vo. 1s. 6d.

[*Elementary Classics.*

MACMILLAN AND CO., LONDON.

www.ingramcontent.com/pod-product-compliance
Lightning Source LLC
Chambersburg PA
CBHW020611030726

47497CB00007B/2193